Murder at Mile Marker 18

A Mallory Beck Cozy Culinary Caper
(Book 1)

Denise Jaden

Denise Jaden Books

Copyright

No part of this book may be reproduced in any form or by any electronic or mechanical means without written permission from the author, except for the use of brief quotations in book reviews. Thank you for respecting this author's work.

This is a work of fiction. Similarities to real people, places, or events are entirely coincidental.

MURDER AT MILE MARKER 18
First Edition. October 20, 2020.
Copyright © 2020 Denise Jaden
Cover Design: Novak Illustration
Cover Illustrations: Ethan Heyde
All rights reserved.
Written by Denise Jaden

Join my mystery readers' newsletter today!

Sign up now, and you'll get access to a special mystery to accompany this series—an exclusive bonus for newsletter subscribers. In addition, you'll be the first to hear about new releases and sales, and receive special excerpts and behind-the-scenes bonuses.

Visit the link below to sign up and receive your bonus mystery:

https://www.subscribepage.com/mysterysignup

Murder at Mile Marker 18

AN UNLUCKY AMATEUR SLEUTH, an adorable cop, and a cat with a hunch...

If anyone had told Mallory Beck she would become Honeysuckle Grove's next unschooled detective, she would have thought they were ten noodles short of a lasagna. Her late husband had been the mystery novelist with a penchant for the suspicious. She was born for the Crock-Pot, not the magnifying glass, and yet here she is elbow deep in fettuccine, cat treats, and teenagers with an attitude, the combination of which lands her smack-dab in the middle of a murder investigation.

Maybe she should have thought twice about delivering a casserole to a grieving family. Maybe she should have avoided the ever-changing green eyes of her seventh-grade crush—now the most heart-stopping cop in town. Maybe she should have stopped listening to the insightful mewls of her antagonistic cat, Hunch, who most likely wants her to be the town's next murder victim.

Whatever the case, Mallory Beck got herself into this investigation, and she has a distraught teenage girl counting on her to deliver the truth.

Start now to help Mallory unravel the mystery...

Dedication
To Shelly,
my first and most loyal reader, who has supported and encouraged me through every draft of every book.

Chapter One

THE WIFE OF A war correspondent or a fighter pilot or even a venomous snake milker (yes, there is such a thing) might expect to be a widow at twenty-eight, but certainly not the wife of a novelist.

And yet here I was, learning how to live life in the oversized house, in a small West Virginia town we settled into only a year ago—alone. To be fair, I hadn't done much in the way of living in the last eight months since Cooper died, but after an offhand comment from my sister about me being under great threat of becoming a cat lady, I was determined to start today.

Being a cat lady wouldn't be so bad if the cat I'd inherited didn't loathe me.

I swung my legs out of Cooper's black Jeep and did a little hip shimmy to straighten my skirt as I stood. Picking out clothes this morning had been about as difficult as choosing between cake and pie (no one should ever have to make that choice). What does one wear that says, *I'm fine, just fine, and I haven't been moping around my dark house for the last eight months, nope, not me, but nonetheless, please, keep your distance?*

Even though it was the middle of August, I had settled on a black skirt with the tiniest of polka dots and a light cornflower blue blouse with matching pumps and a headband that pulled my in-need-of-a-trim bangs back. It didn't spell out the last eight months of my life, but it did the job in making me feel tidy and unapproachable. My coffee-brown hair fell halfway down my back now, full of split ends, but it actually didn't look half bad today for how many months it had been matted against my living room couch.

I strode for the church, the same one I hadn't stepped foot inside since Cooper's memorial service. Church had always been Cooper's thing. I'd gone along to play the part of the good wife but didn't spend too much time considering how I felt about God or how He felt about me. At least I hadn't before He decided to snatch my husband from me.

Two greeters in their mid-forties stood at the closest open glass doors—a man in a gray suit and a woman in an apricot summer dress. Thankfully, I didn't recognize either of them. I'd chosen this as my first big public outing because, at more than three hundred people, I figured our church was the one place I might get in and out of completely unnoticed. As I approached the greeters, though, the woman leaned into the man and whispered something.

I gulped. Apparently, this was how it would go: People would recognize me, remember Cooper, and not know what to say. Why, again, had I gotten out of bed this morning? There had to be at least one Netflix series I hadn't binged yet.

The woman at the door pasted on a bright smile as she turned back to me, just in time to say, "Good morning."

"Good morning," I murmured back, but my voice came out hard and crusty, like bread out of a too-hot oven, or like I hadn't used it in more than a week. Come to think of it, other than talking on the phone with my sister, I probably hadn't.

My tone, at least, had the desired effect, and the greeters let me pass without another word.

My next goal was to make it through the lobby and into the sanctuary without garnering any other stares or attention. This part was not easy. All eyes followed me as I entered the church lobby, and I was pretty sure I wasn't just imagining it.

My late husband, Cooper Beck, had been a well-known mystery writer, so I was used to recognition. After only five years, I hadn't been married long enough to get used to this feeling of notoriety, and I guess I had assumed it would have died with Cooper.

Apparently not so. And not only that, but every single person nearby was scanning my body, probably taking in my too-bright cornflower blouse and thinking it inappropriate for someone in mourning, or noticing the tiny polka dots on my skirt, or wondering why I still wore black after so many months, or...something.

While I was lost in my warring thoughts, Donna Mayberry spotted me, at first only giving me a glance, and I thought I might make it into the sanctuary before actually having to speak to her. But then she did a double take, quickly followed by the head tilt of pity. By this point, I knew that look well. That look was why I had taken to grocery shopping and running errands at midnight instead of during the day like a normal person. At midnight, I could safely avoid the head tilt of pity.

"Mallory Beck?" Donna called with an arm straight up in the air, so any stray person in the vicinity who hadn't yet set eyes on me might do so now. "It's so nice to see you out!" she said loudly, calling public attention to my self-imposed isolation in only two seconds.

Donna had the kind of long legs that would be impossible to outrun. In fact, I blinked, and she was right there beside me. Donna was long everywhere—from her fingers to the dark, shiny hair that fell past her waist. She wore a summery yellow dress that touched the floor, and I had to wonder what kind of a store made clothes that would look long on someone like nearly six-foot Donna. Whether it was her hair or her stature or her clothes, though, Donna Mayberry always seemed to have a way of making me feel frumpy and underdressed.

Then again, maybe all these people would finally look at her instead of me.

Donna and Marv were one of the first couples Cooper and I had met when we'd settled into Honeysuckle Grove a year ago, and while Marv worked about sixteen hours a day, Donna naturally excelled at everything from shrub carving to Michelangelo-inspired nail design, and seemed to have a little too much time on her hands—time to know everything about everyone.

"How are you doing, honey? Is this your first time back at church?" Again with the head tilt of pity. Even though I doubted Donna could know I hadn't left my house in thirteen days, somehow her tone confirmed she absolutely did.

"First time, yes," I replied. No point in denying it.

She angled me away from the imposing stares and nudged me toward an alcove as though she could sense how much the staring bothered me. A second later, a tall, potted plant concealed us in the corner of the lobby, and I had just let out a breath of relief when Donna suddenly started pulling at my skirt.

I grabbed for my skirt and looked down in horror. Was Donna trying to undress me? Was this a bad dream? Maybe I was still sleeping soundly—or as soundly as one could beside a hostile cat while dreaming about being undressed in public.

But as I blinked and then blinked again, Donna held up a pair of beige control-top pantyhose she had peeled off the outside of my skirt to show me. A second later, she tucked them into the outside pouch of my gray leather purse.

"Oh!" I let out a loud noise, something between a yelp and a laugh. "Thank you!"

As I peeked around the plant, it seemed everyone had lost interest in us, thank goodness.

"Well, you'll have to sit with us." Donna straightened her own dress and looked down as though something equally embarrassing might have happened to her, but I was pretty sure we both knew that wasn't how the universe worked. I doubted Marv was here, so "us" likely meant Donna's gossip posse—that was what Cooper and I used to call them—but as Donna tugged my arm toward the far side of the lobby, a jolt of panic shot through me.

"Oh, I can't," I said, pulling away from her eight-tone sunset nails. "I'm, um, meeting someone, and I said I'd be sitting on this side." The first lie I could think of launched off my tongue. I just couldn't imagine sitting with Donna's posse and having them all whisper, "Yes, but how are you really doing?" fifty times throughout the service.

Donna looked to either side of me as though she might regard this mysterious person I could be waiting for. I could have continued with the lie. Said my sister was in town or conjured an imaginary friend or something to put her mind at rest. But I was suddenly just so tired from all of this interaction—the most I'd endured in eight months—and so I simply stood there staring at Donna like my brain had taken an extended vacation.

Eventually, she said, "Oh. Okay then. If you're sure?"

I nodded as she backed away, leaving me to my social anxiety.

A few more head tilts greeted me as I took my seat near the back of the sanctuary on the right, nice and close to the door. Thankfully, my chosen outfit—sans the sticky pantyhose—did its duty of keeping me mostly unapproachable. The church had rarely filled to capacity when Cooper and I had attended, so I had some confidence I'd have the back bench to myself. The only time I'd actually seen this place full was at Cooper's memorial service, but most of those were mystery fans and people fascinated with death, not people who had actually known him.

Soon, the service started with singing and then the pastor's invitation for people to donate and volunteer in any area they were able. Nothing had changed in eight months, apparently. Honeysuckle Grove Community Church still didn't have enough money in the building fund or enough people to host small group Bible studies in their homes. It seemed so very odd that while my life had been turned on its head, leaving me without a husband or a profession, every person around me seemed like a walking robot, pre-programmed for a life that would remain constant until their pre-determined time of death.

As though Pastor Jeff could read my mind, he started his sermon with, "We are not robots."

That was one thing I'd forgotten about church. Pastor Jeff had a great gift for storytelling. He usually started one of his stories with a bold and unusual statement, and then went on a long rabbit trail about his son's first crack at baseball or about that time he lost his luggage in a Taiwanese airport, but then brought it back around to that first bold statement in a way that made the entire congregation think, *Ah, I see what you did there!*

But today, I feared I didn't have the brain capacity to follow his breadcrumbs. He chattered on about what it meant to be part of a family and body parts working together and covering a multitude of sins. At least I had been correct about getting the back bench to myself.

I tuned out for a minute, or maybe it was more than a minute, because the next thing I knew, Pastor Jeff closed his Bible and bowed his head to pray.

I'd done it! I'd made it through the entire service. Okay, maybe I hadn't taken much of it in, but I'd spoken to an actual person, I'd sat here and proved I could act normal, and I hadn't drawn a single bit of attention to myself. Well, besides the part where I wore my pantyhose on the outside of my skirt.

"I'm sorry to have to tell you there's been a recent death in the congregation," Pastor Jeff said. At first, I expected all eyes to once again turn to me, but then quickly realized "recent" in Pastor Jeff's books meant something during the last two seasons. "This past Friday, August the thirteenth, Dan Montrose met his death in an unfortunate accident."

Pastor Jeff resumed bowing his head to pray for the family and their loss. His deep voice boomed with emotion and instantly made me feel like I'd gone back in time eight months. I could physically feel grief for this family I'd never even met, like a two-hundred-pound anchor in my stomach. Pastor Jeff went on to talk about the shock of the death and the wife and children this man had left behind, and because I couldn't bear the weight of the extra grief, I kept my eyes open and focused on our authoritative, if somewhat frazzled, pastor.

Pastor Jeff wore jeans and a beige button-down today. His hair was more in need of a trim than mine, which was saying something, but in every bit of his countenance, he oozed compassion. I wondered how overworked Pastor Jeff must be to take care of such a large congregation. It must involve a lot of stress for someone who cared so much. After Cooper died, Pastor Jeff visited me three times at the house, until I'd finally donned a face that convinced him I was doing fine, just fine, and didn't need a fourth visit. In truth, I probably *did* need that fourth visit, but even then, in the midst of my grief, I had somehow inherently known that I would be doing our overworked pastor a great favor by letting him move on to some other hurting soul within the church.

"Anyone?" Pastor Jeff said, and it took me a second to realize he had finished praying and now gazed over the congregation with his eyes pleading, as he often did at the beginning of the service when asking for volunteers. I had tuned out again. "Can anyone be the arms of this church body and deliver a casserole to these hurting folks, to help out this part of our church family?" He scanned the entire congregation a second time. "It doesn't have to be anything fancy."

He looked to the far side of the sanctuary where Donna and her gossip posse huddled whispering, and then in front of them to where the rest of the church staff sat. The church secretary, Penny Lissmore, let out such a large breath of disappointment, I could see her chest heave from across the large worship center. Pastor Jeff sighed as though admitting defeat to her and explaining telepathically that they'd have to add Casserole Delivery to the long list of things someone on the staff would eventually have to get to.

After Cooper died, I'd had at least a couple of casseroles delivered to me. That time was a bit of a haze, and I definitely didn't ponder at the time how much cajoling it might have taken to get someone to pick up a casserole at the store—they were the store-bought variety, I remembered that much—and bring it over to my house.

I got it. Approaching a grieving widow was probably near the bottom of most people's lists of favorite things to do, right below getting a root canal or having a wardrobe malfunction on your first day back at church. But for the first time, I understood how comforting those little acts of kindness could be.

While I was lost in my thoughts again, I didn't immediately notice the church secretary and an associate pastor look my way, followed by Pastor Jeff. His face broke into a smile that looked as though heaven had just opened and angels were descending right here on this side of the sanctuary.

"Mallory Beck!" he said, and I startled at my name. "I knew I could count on you. Thank you so much, Mallory. The Montrose family will really appreciate this."

I blinked as I clued in to what he was saying. And that's when I realized my hand was high in the air.

Chapter Two

TWO HOURS LATER, I stumbled through my front door, carrying more groceries than one person should be able to manage. As if to prove my point, as I kicked the door shut behind me, the bottom fell out of one of the brown paper bags in my right arm, and dried noodles scattered everywhere.

Hunch peeked around the corner to investigate. Cooper's cat generally snubbed his nose in my direction. Once in a while, he greeted me with a hiss—usually when I was already having a particularly bad day. My sister, Leslie, thought I should really take Hunch down to the SPCA if we didn't get along, but I couldn't get rid of Cooper's beloved cat. Of course I couldn't.

But we also couldn't stand each other.

Now he looked up at me as if saying, "This is new," about not only the noodles on the floor, but also about my overloaded arms. Generally, when I made a trip to the grocery store, I returned with one bag, maybe two. It didn't take a lot to feed a single person, especially one who rarely remembered to eat. Or a single person and a mourning cat.

Yes, mourning. I should take a step back and explain. You see, Hunch was not a normal cat. Hunch's personality was more dog-like than feline in many ways, and he had been every bit the ideal mystery writer's companion. The cat had only ever seemed to enjoy Cooper's company, and I hadn't taken it personally when Cooper was alive because they clearly fit together. When Cooper paced, Hunch paced right alongside him. When Cooper came up with a great plot idea and snapped his fingers, Hunch perched on his haunches right at Cooper's side to high five his owner. I kid you not. Or in this case, would you call it a low five?

I still didn't take Hunch's bristly nature to heart. It just disappointed me that we both missed Cooper terribly and yet we couldn't comfort each other through our grief.

But I could never fill the void Cooper had left in Hunch's life. I couldn't possibly stir up the kind of creative energy that new mysteries and their solutions brought with them. I'd been reading Cooper's novels nonstop for six months to keep what little he'd left behind close to me, and all it had taught me was that I'd lost someone brilliant. No wonder he'd had such a large fan base.

I dropped the intact grocery bags onto the kitchen counter and returned to clean up my mess. Hunch was still investigating, sniffing every inch of my torn grocery bag and its contents like a squatty feline bloodhound. He looked up at me and I swear he raised his eye whiskers on one side as if to ask, "What, exactly, are you up to?"

"I wish I was up to something more exciting," I told Hunch. Cooper had often talked to his cat, but for me, it had always felt strange, at least before today. "Just cooking up a casserole for some nice people who recently experienced a death in the family."

Hunch's fur pricked up on the word "death" and even though there was no story here, no mystery about what I planned to concoct in the kitchen, I figured it wouldn't hurt to let Hunch think differently.

"I'll have to figure out what to do now that I've wasted my noodles," I said, pacing a few times back and forth in our entryway and drumming my fingers on my chin. Hunch watched me for a few seconds. And then he joined me.

The truth was, I knew exactly what to do. And, in fact, purchasing the dried pasta noodles had been a cop-out on my part—barely a step above buying a frozen lasagna.

I didn't blame anyone else for opting for store-bought, of course. Other people had busy lives, while I had absolutely nothing on my agenda, besides getting out of bed and pouring a bowl of cat kibble. Also, most other people didn't have a culinary degree.

Half an hour later, my oven pinged to let me know it was preheated, but I still hadn't decided on a recipe. I had all the ingredients for a basic pasta recipe, but basic seemed much too boring when I hadn't had the opportunity to cook for anyone in eight months. I'd bought tomatoes, so I could flavor the pasta that way, but it still didn't seem good enough. Why hadn't I picked up some spinach? Maybe some saffron?

It ended up being three days and four trips to the grocery store later when I finally decided on a recipe I was happy with. I'd fried sauces and taste-tested a dozen different cheeses. I knew beyond any doubt that I was putting far too much thought into this, and yet I couldn't seem to stop myself.

Besides, once the casserole was cooked, that meant I had to actually deliver it.

But by Wednesday, I had finally worked up the courage and got out of bed by seven in the morning to get started—a time of the day I hadn't seen in many months.

Once again, I preheated the oven, mixed eggs, flour, and salt, and separated my dough into three balls. I blended my first ball with a dough hook and a cup of pureed spinach, the second with crushed tomato, and the third with some olive oil and a touch of saffron. By the time I rolled them all out onto my counter and sliced them into thin fettuccine noodles, I was perfectly pleased with the bouquet of edible colors.

Hunch had been lying on his chair at the kitchen table, chin on his paws, since I started. His eyes followed me throughout the kitchen as I asked myself questions aloud about my recipe and then answered them as if each one were a clue in a grand mystery.

For the first time in eight months, Hunch and I seemed to enjoy each other's company, and all at once, something felt very right about this decision to make a meal for this grieving family. The truth was, I never needed to work again if I didn't want to. Cooper had excellent life insurance, plus a steady stream of royalties from his books. But therein lay the problem—I didn't want to go back to working in a bustling kitchen, and yet I terribly missed cooking, as it never seemed worth putting much effort into the process for only one person. It would be so much easier to stop sitting around my big, lonely house, moping all day every day, if I had somewhere to be.

And now for at least one afternoon, I did.

I continued to ask questions aloud, like, "I wonder how the man died," and "I wonder how his wife is dealing with her grief," as I heated some oil in a saucepan over medium heat, to keep Hunch's attention. I warmed my crushed garlic in the oil until fragrant, added more freshly boiled and crushed tomatoes, and salt. By the time the sauce thickened, I had some chopped basil ready to add.

I grated some cheddar and tried it with the sauce, but quickly decided it lacked richness and added some gorgonzola. Then I layered the casserole into my best white casserole dish—pasta in three different-flavored mounds, then the sauce, a little extra sea salt, and finally the mixture of grated cheeses. I decorated the top with chopped green and yellow peppers for color.

I popped it into the oven and set it to bake twenty-five minutes. And then I raced upstairs to choose an outfit for today's special outing.

Chapter Three

BY ELEVEN O'CLOCK THAT morning, I stood on the doorstep of a sprawling cornstalk-yellow mansion in the upscale Hillcrest neighborhood of Honeysuckle Grove. Cooper had bought us a large house when we had moved to town—large enough, we'd thought, to fill with a boatload of children one day—but it was situated in the flats and nothing like this mountain of a house.

A four-car garage sat off to the left, with mature trees lining a walkway on either side of the expansive yard, but I headed for the ten-foot-wide marbled steps that led to the front door.

When I'd said goodbye to Hunch from our doorstep, he had been sitting on his haunches in the entryway, and I suspected he would be in that same exact position when I returned, eager to hear what I'd discovered during my outing.

The doorbell let out three long chimes when I pressed on it. A moment later, the heavy oak door creaked open, and a maid with flawless bronze skin stood on the other side. The maid wore an actual bonnet and one of those old-fashioned black dresses with a white apron, but her dress ended mid-thigh—shorter than I'd ever seen on any kind of uniform. With long, dark lashes and high cheekbones, the lady was very pretty and had great legs, so it wasn't surprising she'd want to show them off.

"Um, hi." I held out the casserole, hoping my gesture might say it all, as my casual conversational ability hadn't returned since Cooper's death. But the maid just stood there, staring at me with a blank expression. "I'm delivering a casserole on behalf of Honeysuckle Grove Community Church?" I asked it as a question because now that I thought about it, did these people need or even want my delicately prepared dish if they had a maid and probably a cook who could prepare anything at their whim?

Still, I reasoned, maybe the act of kindness would mean something, even to folks with an unlimited supply of money. You never knew.

I held out the casserole another inch toward the maid and said, "Is Mrs. Montrose at home?" All I'd gotten out of Pastor Jeff in the small amount of conversation I could endure Sunday morning was a last name and an address.

"You know the family?" Her blank stare persisted.

I shifted uncomfortably. "Um, no. Not exactly. I was just bringing this by..."

Quite suddenly, she spun and walked into the mansion, leaving the door wide open. As she strode off, she said, "I see if I find her. There is a *velatorio*—a wake on right now, you know."

I sucked in a breath. I hadn't known. From the sounds of the woman, a stranger delivering a casserole at this moment was about as inappropriate as bringing a carton of cigarettes to a cancer patient's first chemo treatment. I was torn between racing my casserole back to my vehicle or placing the dish somewhere just inside the doorway before escaping.

Before I'd known these people were wealthy, I'd decided to use a casserole dish Cooper and I had gotten as a wedding gift, figuring the gesture would force me on another outing to come and retrieve it. But I knew without a doubt that I would never show up on *this* doorstep again in search of my beloved casserole dish. When I tried to picture it, all I could envision was me, draped in rags, holding out my hands, and saying, "Please, ma'am? Alms for the poor?"

The image should have made the decision easy. *Back away and save the casserole for yourself, Orphan Mallory.* But I was having trouble doing that, and before I could force myself to retreat down the steps, another lady stood in the open doorway.

"Mrs. Montrose?" I asked. All this internal debating had made me breathless.

"Yes?" This lady's face bloomed into a bright smile, and again I doubted whether or not I had the right house, the right family. The lady wore her auburn hair in a big bouffant, like something out of the sixties, but her cream-colored, perfectly-tailored dress looked modern. The cream color made me pause again. Could this truly be the wife of the deceased?

But more than my curiosity, self-consciousness consumed me as I stood there in my khaki capris with a sleeveless floral blouse that was tied at the waist. My dress was more than inappropriate for a wake.

"I'm so sorry if this is poor timing," I said and, as hard as I fought it, found my head tilting at her. "I'm delivering a casserole on behalf of Honeysuckle Grove Community Church?" As I said the words, a familiarity developed. Had I seen this lady at church before? It had been so long since I'd been a regular attendee, I couldn't be sure.

"Oh, how lovely," the woman said, her smile brightening even more. "Please, do bring it in and put it on the dining table." She opened the door wider. As I stepped inside, she glanced down at the steam-obscured lid and asked, "Does it have gluten? Or dairy?"

I gulped and stopped in place. I stalled, slipping out of my ballet flats as Cooper and I had been in a habit of doing since buying our new home. "Oh. I'm afraid it has both," I finally said.

When I had worked in various restaurants in the city, they had always listed gluten- and dairy-free options on the menu. It helped with the awkwardness of having to revamp recipes. Allergies hadn't even occurred to me during this morning's cooking spree.

Mrs. Montrose moved deeper into the house. I glanced down and noticed she'd left her shoes on, which, now that I thought about it, was probably more common for a wake, wasn't it?

"No matter, the kids will eat it." Mrs. Montrose waved a casual hand back at me as I debated between putting my shoes back on or leaving them behind. I left them behind for fear she'd lose me in her massive house. I was already dressed completely wrong. What was the difference if I was barefoot? As she continued to lead the way, she murmured, "And if they don't eat it, the greedy, bloodsucking leeches will," so low that I didn't know if I was meant to hear it.

Mrs. Montrose led me through an open room filled with mourners—all dressed in black with either what looked like a mimosa or a fancy canapé in hand—and through to a dining room filled with more food than I had ever seen in one place—and I had worked in more than one restaurant!

The oversized dining room table didn't have an inch of free space. Mrs. Montrose surveyed it quickly, flashed another smile back at me, and said, "Not to worry, I'll call Lupe to help. Lupe?" She pushed through a swinging door and returned a second later with the short-skirted maid on her heels. "Please help Miss...?"

This seemed like an opportunity to be an ear of understanding to these people, so I took it. "Actually, it's Mrs.," I said. "Mrs. Mallory Beck. You see, I also lost my—"

"Do find a place for Mrs. Beck's lovely dish," Mrs. Montrose told her maid, already leaving the dining room to return to her guests.

By the time I had watched her go, I turned back to find that Lupe-the-maid had cleared the perfect spot for my casserole dish. She reached for it, potholders and all, placed it down, and removed the lid. Steam swirled up from within it, and I sighed happily at the cheesy aroma. But as I looked around at the dining room, empty of people other than the two of us, I wondered if it would even get to be enjoyed while it was still warm.

Before I could thank her, Lupe had whisked the lid and potholders toward the kitchen, and as soon as I was left alone, I felt more than awkward. Why on earth had Pastor Jeff thought these people needed a casserole? And delivered by someone who was *actually* in mourning, no less?

I looked over the table, filled with shrimp rolls and zucchini parmesan and slices of triple-layer tuxedo cake, and tried to decide if I was hungry. The least I could get out of this task was a decent meal, and it wasn't as though anyone was around to see me help myself.

But I sighed and decided against it. Even if I thought I was hungry now, one or two bites in, and I'd realize I wasn't.

I headed back for the foyer. Not a single black-clad person looked my way as I slunk through the front room, not even Mrs. Montrose, whose cream-colored dress stood out against the sea of black. She was currently being jabbered at by a skinny man with dark slicked-back hair in a three-piece dark suit. As I passed, I heard him say, "We need to hire somebody ourselves, find the car that hit him, and sue the pants off the guy."

The man winked twice at Mrs. Montrose. At first, I thought he was trying to send her some kind of a secret signal like Marty Sims, the protagonist in Cooper's mystery series might have done, but after he did it again, I realized I'd only been reading too many of Cooper's novels. It was clearly a tic.

I moved through the open room toward the foyer with my mind still on mystery novels. I hadn't heard how the man of the house—Dan Montrose—had died, but from the sounds of things, it was an accident where the other driver had fled the scene. If it had been a murder, who would be the culprit? The maid in the short skirt? The radiant and beaming wife of the deceased? Or the mysterious man in the three-piece-suit who had a tic?

Maybe I wouldn't be so bad at concocting my own mysteries, after all. At the very least, I could entertain Cooper's cat.

Just inside the foyer, I stopped in place. A lady stood in my path. She wore a simple black skirt with a matching billowy blouse and stood facing away, holding a photograph of what must have been Dan Montrose. I could immediately tell by her shoes—a JC Penny black pump with scuffs on the heels—that she wasn't as wealthy as most of this crowd.

I didn't want to retreat into the open room of people, but I also couldn't get to my own pair of lone coral flats I'd kicked off without asking this lady to move. I figured that was the lesser of the two uncomfortable options and cleared my throat. The woman turned to reveal her tear-streaked, familiar face.

"Beth?" I asked at the same time she said, "Mallory Beck?"

Beth Dawson had been our realtor when Cooper and I looked for our first house in Honeysuckle Grove.

I looked again from the photo in her hands to Beth's tear-streaked face. "I'm so sorry," I said—the one phrase I swore I'd never say to a grieving person, as it didn't help one bit. I quickly covered with, "How did you know the, um, deceased?"

Beth nodded and placed the photo back onto the foyer's narrow oak table. "He was my sister's husband. It's just awful what happened."

"Oh? Your sister is Mrs. Montrose?" I could see the resemblance now. Beth wore her auburn hair closer to her head and donned a fair bit less makeup, although she clearly wore some, as it had streaked around her eyes.

"Yes, Helen is my sister," she said, and the statement seemed loaded with...something. Underlying emotion? Years of sisterly fights over shared clothes and competing for boys?

This thought made me immediately piece together the fact that Mrs. Helen Montrose seemed perfectly fine after her husband's very recent death—only five days ago—while her sister was quite broken up about it.

I had to comment. "It seems like your sister is holding herself together quite well."

Beth twisted her lips and tilted her head. I wasn't entirely sure what the look meant, but then she went on to say, "You know who's really hurting over Dan's death? The children. They haven't been eating, don't want to talk to me or to Helen, and haven't even come out of their rooms all day."

I put a hand to my chest, physically hurt from the thought of how much his children must be suffering. I glanced down at my lone pair of flats, which someone—probably Lupe—had aligned neatly beside a wooden coatrack. But now I didn't want to leave. Helen Montrose didn't want my help and comfort, but perhaps someone in this household did.

"Do you think it would be okay if I brought the kids a plate of food to their rooms?" I asked Beth. Being their aunt, she would know if this was inappropriate. "I just brought a fresh casserole."

Beth smiled. "You know, they'd probably love that. I think they're tired of everyone they know asking them if they're all right. I promised I'd give them their space today, but I hate knowing they're not getting anything to eat."

I smiled. "Where do I find their bedrooms?"

"Right up the stairs from the dining room. Come on, I'll show you."

Before she turned to lead the way, I said, "Wait," and dug into my purse for a tissue. I pulled one out of a package and handed it to her, motioning to her eyes.

She smiled her thanks, and a second later, Beth was tidied up and leading me back through the open room of people. Not a single person looked away from their conversations to us. Lupe wove around the room with a tray of canapés, which made it clear why the dining room was so deserted. Apparently, these people didn't retrieve their own food.

As we moved through to the dining room, I asked Beth, "I overheard something earlier, and, well...Was your brother-in-law killed in a car accident, a hit-and-run?"

Beth let out a long sigh. "That's what they tell us, yes. Where did you hear that?"

A rush of heat traveled up my neck for having been caught eavesdropping. "Oh, well, I had just been about to say goodbye to your sister, and a man was telling her he wanted to find the car who hit Dan and sue him, or something like that."

Beth nodded and slipped a tendril of shoulder-length auburn hair behind her ear. "That would be Terrence Lane. He's another lawyer at the firm where Dan was a partner." She shook her head. "I'd heard there wasn't much chance of finding the person responsible. If Terrence can, I'm all for it."

If the person took off, it seemed as though there had to be a way to find the person so he or she could at least be held accountable for that.

But Beth sighed again. "I supposed it wouldn't bring Dan back, regardless. This family has enough money, and I'm sure the person already feels awful. So what's the point? Why not just let everyone get past their grief and move on with their lives."

She didn't ask it as a question, and so I didn't answer. I couldn't say I agreed with her. If Cooper's death hadn't so clearly been an accident, if there had been any mystery hanging over the fire at the bank, about why it had happened or who was at fault, I would not have been able to think about anything else.

Although, I guess that was true anyway.

"Oooh, that looks good," Beth said, taking my attention and pointing to my casserole. "Amber loves melted cheese."

I reached for one of the untouched plates and dug a heaping scoop out of the casserole dish. Then I decided I should really include a small mound of each type of pasta. It would mess up the appearance of the rest of the casserole, but it wasn't like that mattered too much in the empty dining room. "And Amber is the Montrose daughter, I assume?"

"Yes. She's fifteen and has been pretty upended about the whole thing."

"No doubt. Is she the oldest?"

Beth shook her head. "Danny Jr. Or I guess he's going by his middle name, Seth, lately. He's seventeen. He's been really angry. I don't know if he'd take any food, but you could try."

Her tone didn't sound hopeful, but nevertheless, I reached for another plate and filled it with an extra-large helping of pasta. I'd heard that teenage boys could eat. Soon I had two beautiful, appetizing tri-colored pasta plates ready for delivery.

"Right up there," Beth said, pointing up a set of stairs. "Danny's room is at the top of the stairs. Amber's is halfway along on the right."

"Okay, thanks. You're sure you don't want to come along?" Now that I was actually making a move toward the stairs, awkwardness consumed me. I didn't know these people, after all.

Beth lifted her flat palms up to face me. "No, no. I'm giving them their space. Oh, and I should warn you, if Danny's friend Cade is with him, you might just want to leave them be."

I was already on the second stair, but I turned back. "Yeah? Why's that?"

Beth shook her head as she headed for the kitchen. "When those two get together, they're never up to any good."

Chapter Four

I'D BARELY MADE IT to the top of the stairs when I made out two male voices through an almost closed door. Great. What had I gotten myself into? I certainly didn't want to insert myself into the middle of two troublemaking teens.

I paused on the top stair for a second, rethinking that. Or did I?

I didn't have children, although Cooper and I had been eager to have them, just as soon as he finished the last book in his latest series and I worked my way up to sous-chef, so I could forever have that title on my resume. It didn't happen, obviously, but I did understand troubled teens. In fact, I had been one.

Dad had moved us around a lot after Mom left. Six months here, two months there. I'd even lived in Honeysuckle Grove for a short stint in seventh grade. It was why the town had been on my radar and I'd suggested it to Cooper as a place to settle down. Here, more than anywhere, felt like home when I'd been a young girl. But Dad had said it didn't suit us, and after nearly a year, when I'd only just started to let out my breath, he told us we were moving again.

I'd been in high school when I realized he'd been lying about every single one of those moves. The towns had suited us just fine. He'd just been lazy and irresponsible and couldn't hold a job.

So out of anyone, I understood angry teenagers. And now, hovering on the top step, I recognized the tone one hundred percent.

"You're sure it's okay I'm here?" one voice asked. I had to guess it was Cade, as Danny Jr.—or Seth—lived here.

"Sure," the other voice said, his voice all gravel and spite. "My dad's dead, like you wanted. Who's going to stop you? My mom wouldn't care if we stayed in here and played Call of Duty for the next year."

Whoa. I took a step back on the stairs, nearly tripping when Cade said, "Dude, you wanted him dead as much as I did."

This was a whole new level of angry teenager. Sure, I had been mad at my dad, even hated him at times. But I never would have wished him dead.

"So you're not even going to college now that your dad's not around to make you?" Cade went on. "What about the deposit?"

"Ha. Who cares now?" the Montrose son replied. "Mom's going to get a huge insurance settlement and she won't care if I spend the next four years working on the 'Vette. It's Dad who was making me go, making me keep up my grades. Now that he's out of the picture, I can do what I want. Maybe I'll even become a mechanic."

I looked down at the two plates in my hands, deciding in an instant that I might be hungry after all. I'd just take one plate to Amber first.

I tiptoed past Danny's room and tried to remember the directions Beth Dawson had given me. Halfway down on the right?

Thankfully, a door down the hall was open a few inches. Through the gap, I could see a teenage girl stretched out on her bed. I balanced one plate on my arm and knocked with two knuckles.

"Yeah?"

I nudged the door open and extended the fuller plate of casserole toward her. "I brought you some food?"

Her eyebrows pulled together, distrust evident, but the girl was immediately familiar. I had definitely seen this girl at church, probably more than once by how familiar she seemed. She wore jeans and an oversized lime green sweatshirt that read *I'M NOT ALWAYS SARCASTIC—SOMETIMES I'M SLEEPING*. She had the same auburn hair as her mother and aunt, but hers was curly and cut short into a pixie cut.

"I'm from Honeysuckle Grove Community Church and was asked to bring by a casserole." The girl still didn't say a word or even beckon me and the food toward her, so I felt the need to fill the silence. "I lost my husband eight months ago. I guess that's why they asked me to deliver this."

This explanation was definitely stretching the truth, but Amber's look softened, and it sounded a lot better than *I volunteered because no one else would, and I didn't want to see Pastor Jeff begging on his knees.*

"Oh. Okay. Thanks." Amber had a soft, vulnerable face with rounder cheeks and fuller lips than her mom, but I could see how this young face might become hardened to look more like her mother's over time.

I brought her a plate of casserole. "No allergies?" I asked as I passed it over.

One side of Amber's lip turned up slightly as she shook her head. I was referring to her mother's probably long list of food intolerances, and thankfully she seemed to take my question as a lighthearted joke.

"I'm Mallory, by the way. Mallory Beck."

She finally reached for the plate and one of the forks I'd brought along from the dining room table. Without looking up, she took a bite. Then another. And then two more.

"This is really good," she said through a full mouth. Finally, she looked up, glanced at the plate in my other hand, and said, "There's a chair by my desk."

I opened my mouth to tell her the other plate had actually been for her brother, but then closed it quickly. If this grieving girl was inviting me to stick around, who was I to argue?

"So how did your husband die?" she asked when I'd just sat down and taken my first bite of melted cheese. It ended up going down the wrong way and causing me to sputter and choke. I put my plate on her nearby desk, which was neat as a pin with makeup and books so precisely lined up along each side, it looked like they had been measured with a ruler.

I coughed into my elbow, but then Amber said, "Hands up," and demonstrated, lifting her arms high in the air. I followed suit. I coughed just a couple more times, and she added, "Don't die on me now," which made me want to start choking all over again.

I'd somehow made it through the last eight months successfully avoiding talking to anyone about the details of Cooper's death. Of course that could have had something to do with the abandoned grocery carts I'd left in my wake upon seeing familiar faces at the grocery store or sitting in the most remote of church pews. But this young girl asking me about him now, as shocking as it was, also somehow felt...refreshing.

"Do you remember hearing about the snow that collapsed on some old wiring and started a fire at the bank on Fifth Street last winter?" Honeysuckle Grove was on the large side of being a small town. Even if I had lived here my entire life, I had doubts if I would be chummy with most people in town, and certainly not this affluent family. However, the bank fire had made headlines for weeks.

So it didn't surprise me when Amber's eyebrows pulled together and she drew out the word, "Yeah," as though hoping I wasn't going to say what came next.

"My husband, Cooper, had been at that bank. He'd been in the safety deposit vault and was one of three people who didn't make it out before the whole thing went up in flames."

Amber's eyes went wide. I braced for her *I'm sorry*, but instead, she only nodded. After a long minute of nodding, she said, "I bet you had questions after it happened, huh?" I couldn't coax any words right away, so Amber went on. "Like why it had to happen while he was in there, why not half an hour before or half an hour after? Or why was he one of the people who didn't make it out alive?"

I had asked all of those questions countless times, along with many others. The police and building inspector had thoroughly explained the unfortunate combination of bad weather and ancient wiring that had caused the accident, and yet a loop of these questions kept swirling in my mind, even eight months later. Now, listening to Amber ask each question with such passion, as though she was asking them about her own dad, I realized maybe all of the questioning was simply human nature.

Because I still couldn't bring myself to speak on the subject, Amber went on. "Did you go there after? To the bank? Did you see it?"

With three pointed questions, I had no choice but to coax an answer. Either that or run out of here like a frazzled chicken. "I, um, yeah, I did. There wasn't much to see, but I had to look at where he died." It had been a mess of charred beams and gaping holes. I'd heard the bank had received a facelift since then, but I hadn't had any desire to see its new finish.

Amber's chin jutted out, and I instantly sucked in my bottom lip like I'd said something wrong. "See?" Her eyes widened. "Mom says it's morbid to want to go out to where it happened, that I'll have nightmares, and I need to just move on and forget about the horrible accident. Yeah, right. I'll just forget about Dad's death, pretend it never happened. Paste on a smile and say, 'Accident? What accident?'" There was the sarcasm her sweatshirt had promised. Amber's face implored me, begging me to see the similarity.

And although she was only fifteen and I truly had no place here in the midst of this family's decisions as they grieved their father and husband, I couldn't help myself. I understood Amber's viewpoint completely. What if I had been forbidden to visit the bank property where Cooper had died? What if I'd been too young to have a driver's license and get myself there?

"And he didn't just die *anywhere*," she went on, setting her half-full plate on her nightstand so she could add to the passion of what she was saying by holding out her hands. "It was on the Old Mission Highway, toward Maryland."

I shook my head slowly, wondering if that was supposed to mean something. If it did, I wasn't following. I'd heard of the Old Mission Highway, but I wasn't sure I'd ever driven on it.

Thankfully, Amber went on to explain. "It's this tiny old highway leading out of town. My parents got married along there, in a big green space right near Big Bear Lake Camplands. Then, because they got married on May the fifth, they drove out to Mile Marker 5 and carved their initials into a tree on the side of the road. A few years ago on my birthday, Dad drove me out to Mile Marker 27 and helped me carve my initials there, because I was born on December twenty-seventh."

I was momentarily distracted, thinking how awful it would be as a kid to have a birthday so close to Christmas. But Amber stood, her arms out, imploring me to pay attention to what she was telling me.

"So he liked to mark the mile markers along that highway of important events?" I asked slowly, keeping my eyes on hers as though that might help me understand.

Then she finally said the sentence that made it all click into place. "You could say that. The most important event of his life—his death—happened right at Mile Marker 18, and no one will even talk about it!"

I squinted and tilted my head, wondering if this all could be true. Her eyes stayed locked on mine, serious, determined. Why would her mother be so tight-lipped about her dad dying in such a significant place?

And so even though I knew it was wrong if her mother had discouraged it, I placed my own pasta plate aside and asked Amber, "Do you want me to take you out there?"

Amber took two giant steps toward me and grabbed my hand. "Are you kidding me? Yes!"

If Helen Montrose found out, she had the money to make sure I got into big trouble over this, but even so, I stood and pulled out my keys to show her I wasn't kidding at all.

Chapter Five

BEFORE WE HEADED FOR the door, I insisted Amber leave a note for her mom. We switched places—she took the desk chair and I sat back on her plush cream-on-white bedspread, while we came up with a reasonable story about how she went for a walk to visit a neighborhood dog that she loved.

As Amber wrote, I surveyed her room. Even the tiniest of items were in their place. As a teenager, my room had usually contained mere glimpses of visible floor space beneath discarded clothes and schoolbooks, so we definitely were not alike in that regard. A pair of men's muddy shoes stood out, aligned just outside of her closet, along with a black garbage bag. Before I had a chance to ask about them, Amber started talking.

"Mom's allergic to cats, dogs, anything with dander," she explained while writing her note. Her voice had taken on a lightness I hadn't heard in it before, and I felt as though the opportunity to get some closure over her dad's death was definitely something she needed. "To tell you the truth, I think she just doesn't like animals. So she doesn't bother me when

I need to get my fix with Tinkerbell down the street. And she would never, ever come looking for me while I was doing it."

Our next problem was getting out of the house without raising the attention of any of Amber's family or the wake-goers. Amber assured me she had done this many times.

"If you knew my parents' friends, you'd know they're pretty wrapped up in themselves. You'd have to spell out 'We're doing something wrong here' for them to even blink an eye."

Even though Amber tromped loudly and spoke in a normal tone as we passed her brother's room, I couldn't help but tiptoe.

Seth clearly wasn't as self-absorbed as his parents' friends. He swung his door open when we'd barely made it to the stairs. He looked between his sister and the twenty-eight-year-old woman tiptoeing toward the stairs behind her. "What's going on? Where are you going?"

Before I could stammer out an excuse, Amber spoke up in a perfectly calm and collected voice. "Don't you and Cade worry your pretty little heads about it."

Seth dropped his voice to a low hiss. "You're going down there? Into the pit of vipers?"

Amber continued her trek down the stairs and called over her shoulder, "Chill, Danny. I'm not going to the wake. Just taking Mom's friend to see Tinkerbell."

This seemed to satisfy Seth—or Danny. I didn't know what to call him now if his sister still called him Danny. But his outburst confused me. Why would her brother care if she went to the wake? Why did he consider his parents' friends to be "vipers," while Amber only saw them as self-absorbed?

"You're going with her?" Danny said to me, an edge to his voice. Much slower on my tiptoes, I had yet to make it past his door. "What do you want? Our money? Amber can't help you with that. Might as well go straight to our mother."

I stopped and turned to the angry boy. His reddish-brown hair stuck up on top and looked out of place with his dark slacks and white button-down. It wasn't as though I lacked compassion. Perhaps a revolving door of adults came in and out of his life, trying to leech onto his family's money. Perhaps this was the only way he knew to protect his sister.

But I had only delivered a casserole, for crying out loud! I didn't deserve the brunt of this.

"Listen, kid," I told him, skipping his name altogether. "I don't want anything from you or your family. I brought a casserole by and heard your sister hadn't been eating. I thought she could use a few minutes out of the house to clear her head." I took a step toward him. "Have you got a problem with that?"

In that second, Danny Jr.'s eyes widened, and he looked like a Danny Jr. He looked like somebody's little boy and not the angst-filled teenager who had been standing there only a second ago. He looked down at the floor and said, "No. 'Course not."

The bedroom door swung open wider behind Danny, and another boy about the same age stood in the doorway. This must be Cade. He, unlike Danny, was not dressed for the occasion in ratty sweatpants and a dirty T-shirt that looked out of place in this swanky mansion. His blond hair was equally unruly.

Cade looked at me with his jaw tight, and with eyes that lacked any emotion, he said, "The guy's dad just died. Cut him a break." He didn't give me a chance for any rebuttal. A second later, he yanked his friend back into his bedroom and slammed the door in my face.

Highly embarrassed for saying all the wrong things, I raced down the stairs and arrived in the dining room, now empty except for Amber. I looked back toward the entry, where I'd left my shoes, but Amber grabbed my hand and pulled me the other way, toward a swinging door.

It led to the kitchen where Lupe busily placed fresh hors d'oeuvres from the oven onto a serving tray. I supposed she was more of a housekeeper than a maid. A teenage boy with tan skin and black hair stood beside her at the counter, doing the same.

"Spread them out," Lupe told the boy, taking absolutely no notice of us. "Make them look fancy."

The boy scowled and murmured, "Gotta be some kinda pompous jerk to notice how spread out the roulettes are." He picked one up and popped it into his mouth.

"Stop it!" Lupe glared at him.

The boy laughed. "Why don't I go ask Helen if I can have some? She thinks I can do no wrong." It didn't seem like a serious suggestion as he resumed placing the roulettes onto the serving tray.

Lupe shook her head and whispered, "Only couple more days."

Unnoticed, Amber pulled me behind them and out through another door. A second later, we stood in a mudroom that was larger than my master bedroom.

"Who was the kid?" I asked, but then realized he was probably older than Amber. Teenagers never liked to be called kids. "I mean, the guy working with your housekeeper?"

Amber rolled her eyes. "That's Lupe's son, Nando. He must have done something wrong to deserve the punishment of helping her. She doesn't make him come here often. My dad never liked him hanging around."

But her mom did, I thought but didn't say. Apparently, Helen Montrose thought the housekeeper's son could do no wrong.

Amber shoved her feet into a pair of white sneakers, crushing the heels until she worked her feet all the way into them.

"Um," I said, looking between our feet.

She looked at me with raised eyebrows. "You're going to look cute out there on the road in bare feet."

I nibbled my lip. "My shoes are at the front entrance."

Amber took a sidelong look at my feet, reached into a shelf, and pulled off another pair of white sneakers. The things were pristine and looked like they had never been worn outside of the house.

I took the sneakers, and although they felt a little snug, at least I wouldn't be in them for long. I glanced back toward the kitchen, glad no one had discovered us. "Let's do this."

Amber led us through another door that opened into their four-car garage. Three bays contained a vehicle, and yet it still felt open and spacious, as though it could easily fit four or five more.

Amber ran a hand along the car closest to us, a maroon sedan. "This was dad's car."

I glanced down at the high-end pristine car, surprised it had been fixed so quickly and completely in five days after a fatal accident.

Before I could ask, she pointed to the second bay. "That's Mom's Tesla." My eyes lingered on the deep metallic blue vehicle. I wasn't much of a car person, but a Tesla would be my dream vehicle. "And that's Danny's." She pointed to an old bright blue Corvette. It had to be a 1970's or 80's model. The wheels had been removed, and it was up on blocks.

"Danny's a mechanic?" I asked, recalling the earlier conversation I'd overheard with Cade.

This made Amber laugh. "Maybe he wished he could be one, but if you ask me, he coulda bought a fully functioning Corvette four times over with the amount he's put into this thing."

Amber didn't give me a chance to ask any more about her dad's car or that beautiful Tesla as she led me out through the far garage door and down the side path toward the street. I glanced both ways, but thankfully, all the wake-goers had remained inside. I hurried down the street to my Jeep.

"Nice ride," Amber said.

Truthfully, I'd always been a small car type of person. My own vehicle was a white Prius. After Cooper died, I don't know what changed, but every time I went out to the driveway, I naturally gravitated toward his Jeep. It had been his baby when I'd first met him. I'd argued that he should trade it in for something a little more environmentally friendly. He'd argued about how driving it made him feel powerful, like he could endure anything that came into his path.

And now here I was, trying to find that feeling and not giving a single thought to the environment.

"Thanks," was all I said. "Now where's this Old Mission Highway?"

Amber directed me toward the outskirts of town, and even though the radio droned some top forty music, it seemed unbearably quiet in the Jeep.

"So you're, what, about sixteen?" I happened to know from her Aunt Beth that Amber was actually fifteen, but in my experience, teenagers always liked to be mistaken for being older.

"Fifteen," she said, a smile fighting at the edges of her lips.

"And so tenth grade?"

"Mmhmm. In September."

And then more silence.

"And your family goes to the community church?"

She snickered. "Only me and Mom—and only because I make her. Dad works—worked," she corrected, "seven days a week, and Danny wouldn't be caught dead in a church."

It made sense now why Amber was the most recognizable.

"What do you do?" Her voice, or maybe just her question, sounded abrupt.

"Oh, me?" Stupid question for the only other person in the vehicle. "I used to work in restaurants. Working my way up to chef."

"That's why that casserole was so good, huh?"

Now I fought a grin. "I'm glad you liked it."

"I always wanted to learn how to cook. Mom said she'd get our housekeeper, Lupe, to teach me, but..." Amber looked out the passenger window.

I much preferred the conversation focus on her future in cooking than on mine, so I pushed. "But?"

Amber shrugged. "Lupe's always treated me and Danny like entitled brats. Dad liked her too much to fire her, probably because she dresses like a tramp." Amber shrugged again, as though this side of her dad was old news. "I'm surprised Mom hasn't canned her yet. It's probably only because she's looking for a new BFF for Danny."

"Lupe's son, Nando?" I asked. I recalled what Lupe had whispered to her son, about only a couple of more days. I wondered if she would be "canned" by the end of the week.

"Yeah, Mom loves him, probably more than she loves us." She snickered, making clear she didn't truly believe this. "Nando just knows how to play adults. He puts on this fake politeness, like he's Mr. Manners or something. Different story when he's around me and Danny."

"So Danny doesn't like him, then?"

Amber shook her head vehemently. "No way."

The Jeep became quiet again. Too quiet. I adjusted my rearview mirror, pausing to make sure I really wanted to make an offer. But just as my hand had shot up in church without my express permission, it was already leaving my mouth. "Maybe sometime I could teach you to cook."

"Yeah?" she asked, and I could feel her eyes boring into the side of my face.

"Sure." I cleared my throat, trying to get my bearings back about having unwittingly planned another social occasion. "I don't think you're entitled. Or a brat." I flashed a smirk in her direction. "Then again, I just met you."

I expected some sort of sarcastic comment in return, but she came back with, "You said used to. What do you do now instead?"

I shifted and adjusted my rearview mirror again to avoid her question, but it only reverberated in the air around us. I didn't think *moping in bed with a cat who wants to claw my eyes out* was a satisfactory answer, so finally I settled on, "Not much."

"That's because of Cooper?" she asked, more bluntly than I expected.

I nodded toward the steering wheel, but thankfully, right then we came upon our destination. Amber pointed. "This is it. Mile Marker 18."

I pulled over and took in my surroundings for the first time. "This? This is where the accident occurred?"

We were at least fifteen miles out of town, and clearly eighteen miles to the state border. I didn't think there were any towns in between. Tall trees lined each side of the pavement with a small shoulder and then a drop-off down a steep bank. The straight road veered only slightly as far as the eye could see in either direction

"That's what the cop said." Amber pointed. "Mile marker 18. I eavesdropped on the whole conversation and made notes." She flashed me the screen of her phone to show me. Sure enough, a small green post with the number 18 indicated our location.

I put the Jeep into park and turned off the engine. No traffic, no dark unexpected corners. It hadn't even rained in the past two weeks. It just didn't look like the site of an accident.

Amber stepped out of the Jeep in an instant and stood in the middle of the road, surveying the location. I wanted to tell her to get off the road, but the truth was, we would see a car in either direction long before it had a chance to get close to her.

By the time I stood beside her, Amber had bent to her knees, inspecting the pavement. "No black tire marks."

I looked down the road in each direction. Perhaps the accident didn't occur exactly in this spot, but then again, the pavement appeared unmarked gray as far as the eye could see. "I don't even see any debris from the cars."

"Car," Amber said.

"What's that?"

"Only one car. There wouldn't be debris, but you'd think there would at least be skid marks."

"One car?" I tilted my head. Had Dan Montrose run into a tree? But, no. I'd heard hit-and-run.

"Yeah, Dad had gotten out of his car when he was hit."

"That's why his car hadn't been damaged?" I surmised.

Amber nodded, seemingly still deep in thought. "Why would he get out of his car way out here in the middle of nowhere?" She marched toward the roadside in front of my Jeep and bent down to study the green mile marker.

Why indeed? But the last thing I wanted to do was give Amber any extra ammunition to dwell on the details of her dad's death. We had come here so she could get some closure.

"Maybe there was something wrong with his car? I'm sure he was trying to hitch a ride back into town and the driver simply didn't see him." As I spoke the words, the explanation felt more plausible.

Amber, however, still didn't look convinced. She moved off the shoulder and ran her hand over the bark of a nearby tree. "But the police brought Mom out here and she drove his car home. There was nothing wrong with it."

"Cars can be unpredictable sometimes, making noises one minute, stopping the next." Even to my own ears, the excuse sounded weak.

But Amber looked like she wasn't even listening. She'd stopped at the second tree she had inspected. Squinting, she moved her face closer, tilting her head. She had both hands on the bark now. "What's FDS?"

"Huh?" I moved over to her side. Sure enough, FDS had been carved into the tree bark. From the darkened, almost black letters, it looked as though it had been carved some time ago—definitely not in the last week. Amber had gotten so quiet, I wondered if she was waiting for my answer.

"I have no idea—" I started to say.

"And why Mile Maker 18? What ever happened on the 18th?" She moved to the nearby trees almost frantically, pawing at all sides of them for more carvings. I searched in the other direction, trying to be of help. I had a feeling that what had been meant to help calm Amber's anxious questions was actually having the opposite effect.

I couldn't find any other carvings, and when I looked back, Amber had disappeared. I moved back to the mile marker and could see flashes of her lime green sweatshirt through the thick of trees and down the steep bank. "Hey, you probably shouldn't—"

"What about his shoes?" she said, in way of an answer.

"His shoes?" She had gone far enough that I had to yell.

"They were muddy when we got them back from the coroner. Even his pant legs were muddy."

I thought back to the muddy shoes that had looked out of place in Amber's pin-neat bedroom. I took in the dry gray road and the dusty shoulder, and it didn't compute. Then I moved a step into the thick knit of trees. From what I could tell, the ground sloped down for about twenty feet and then leveled off to a small creek. Or maybe it was more of a swamp.

"Do you think there's anything to find down...?" I started to ask Amber, but not loud enough that she could hear me. I began climbing down the steep bank, using tree branches for balance. "Careful," I called as I almost lost my balance. I was tempted to turn back, but I couldn't let a fifteen-year-old, who I'd brought out here, let's remember, tumble down the hill alone and injure herself. I had to at least go along.

A dozen steps down the steep bank, I remembered the sterling white shoes I'd borrowed. I looked down, but it was too late. Already stained brown beyond repair, they would be impossible to fully clean. Amber didn't seem to care about her own shoes, now more brown than white, and so I figured I shouldn't be too concerned either.

By the time I reached the swampy creek, Amber stood over a fresh mound of wet dirt. Beyond that, a foot-wide hole had been dug out of the earth.

"It looks like somebody dug something up here." Amber crouched and took some wet dirt into her hand. She felt it between her fingers, as though she'd be able to tell by the consistency who had done the digging and whether or not it was the same dirt that had been on her dad's shoes. If we were in a Cooper Beck novel, and she was Marty Sims, she'd probably be able to.

But Amber was right about one thing: It did look like something had been dug up here, and recently. What were the chances that some random person had been out here in the middle of nowhere at Mile Marker 18, digging up something during the same week that Dan Montrose got out of his car for some unknown reason and was struck to his death?

The chances had to be slim to none.

Chapter Six

THE ENTIRE DRIVE BACK to the Montrose mansion, I tried to keep my suspicions to myself and provide answers to all of Amber's burning questions.

But my answers weren't doing anything to put either of our minds to rest and we both knew it. I pulled over at the end of Amber's street, not wanting to get any closer for fear that a visitor of the wake might see me dropping her off, but Amber didn't get out.

"The cops will never listen to me if I go to them with this," she said, looking straight ahead. "They didn't even want me in the room when they came to talk to Mom about the accident."

Accident. The word suddenly rang out in my head as false. Was it an accident? What was Dan Montrose doing out of his car? Why the carved initials in the tree? Who had dug something up down the bank? Why were there no skid marks? The questions Amber had been asking for the last hour now plagued me as well.

"Would it put your mind at rest if I reported our findings to the police? At the very least, they could look into what might have been dug up, or when the ground might have been tampered with, and how close that was to the actual incident." Calling it an incident felt a little more accurate.

"Yes!" she said, turning toward me, her eyes hopeful and wide. "Let's go."

Oh. I hadn't meant right this second. I also hadn't meant for her to come along with me. But who was I kidding? I wouldn't be able to go home, kick up my feet in front of the TV, and put this out of my mind. I needed answers as much as Amber did.

Twenty minutes later, we pulled into the Honeysuckle Grove Police Department parking lot. We walked up the winding cement walkway, and Amber opened the glass door to the building and held it open for me. Clearly, she appreciated me doing this and didn't think she'd make any headway on her own.

In truth, she probably had a pretty good grasp on her place in all of this. When I had been a teen, I remembered feeling invincible, until that one time when the rug was pulled out from underneath me. Dad grounded me from the car and the phone and then my boyfriend dumped me because I couldn't call him back.

Ahh, the façade of teenage invincibility.

At the busy police department reception desk, we waited for a full five minutes before the receptionist even acknowledged us. It gave me the feeling that even now, as an adult, I held no more power or invincibility than a fifteen-year-old in the greater world, despite driving a power-inducing Jeep for the last eight months.

Finally, the woman in wire-rimmed glasses and a tight bun greeted us. "Yes, can I help you?" She didn't actually sound as though she wanted to be of any help.

"Hi. We'd like to speak to the detective in charge of the Montrose incident, please."

The woman typed into her computer for several long moments, so long I wondered if I should repeat my request. But just as I opened my mouth to do so, she looked up.

"You can share any pertinent information with me, and I'll pass it along."

I'd only just met the woman, but somehow, I didn't believe her. "We'd really prefer to speak directly to the detective in charge." I motioned between Amber and me.

"Our detectives are very busy. Now, is there something else I can do for you?"

I squinted. I'd had very little personal interaction with police or authorities, but I had helped research police procedures for several of Cooper's novels. Back in our college days, when I used to hang out with him at the library, poring over computer logs and reference books, he explained to me that one solid tip would get Marty Sims, his lead detective, into action. The police department would have taken any informant seriously. I'd never had a chance to ask, "Well, what if the receptionist wouldn't allow your informant to get to Marty?"

"I just...can't we talk to someone in charge?" I asked.

The lady raised an eyebrow, and the motion looked painful with her tight bun. It was clear who had the upper hand in the room, and it was not the bumbling twenty-eight-year-old amateur sleuth who was supposed to be helping a young girl find closure.

"This is the daughter of the man who lost his life," I explained, motioning to Amber. Thankfully, she didn't look at all annoyed at me for dragging her into the conversation. If anything, she looked eager. "She really wanted to talk to the detective about the details of the...incident."

The lady's countenance softened. I had the distinct impression that Amber *would* have been much more successful on her own here. "I'm afraid Officer Martinez isn't in the office at the moment," she said to Amber. "But we have counselors in the office if you'd like to sit down with one of them?"

Amber's jaw tightened. "No. Thanks."

"When will Officer Martinez be back?" I asked. It wasn't lost on me that this receptionist had referred to him as an officer and not a detective. It made me wonder if the accident site had been investigated at all.

The lady looked back at me as though I was an annoying gnat she had already swatted out the door once. "I'm afraid I couldn't say."

"Well, can we leave a number so he can call us?" I crossed my arms, trying to find the upper hand, or at the very least a toe's worth of footing in this conversation.

The lady stared hard at me, and then turned to Amber. "What's your number, honey?"

Amber flinched at the endearment but rattled off her phone number in a monotone.

"I'll get one of the counselors to give you a call," the lady said and turned back to her computer as though dismissing us.

Amber flapped her arms up to the sides, and I felt exactly the same way.

"Come on," I said, grabbing her arm and directing her toward the door. "We'll figure something out."

"See? That's exactly what I thought would happen." She stomped down the cement path toward the parking lot, and I hurried to keep up. I wanted to offer some reassuring words, but an equal amount of frustration coursed through me.

Then, suddenly, Amber stopped in place, and her mouth gaped open. I followed her gaze to a man in a police uniform who had just stepped out of a police cruiser.

He started walking our way, his gaze locked on the building behind us, but Amber stopped him with, "Detective Martinez?"

I squinted as she said it, for a couple of reasons. First, because hadn't the receptionist called him *Officer* Martinez? And second, because I knew him.

"It's Officer Martinez," the man grumbled at Amber, as though he had just read my mind. "What can I help you with?"

"I...my dad... did you...?" It was the first time I'd heard Amber at a loss for words. I should have come to her rescue, but I was too stunned to do anything of the sort—stunned and fixated on Xander Martinez.

"I'm sorry?" he asked.

Amber turned to me with wide, pleading eyes. I had to say something, but all that came out of my mouth was, "Xander?"

The officer turned and squinted at me. He looked as handsome as I would have expected from the twelve-year-old Xander Martinez. I wanted to see under his police cap to see how short he kept his dark hair now. It used to be curly on the ends.

He tilted his head, but thankfully, this wasn't the head tilt of pity. "Mallory Vandewalker?"

"Actually, it's Beck now. Mallory Beck." Through all the times Dad moved us around the country, I didn't remember many of my classmates, but Xander stood out in my mind. I'd had a terrible crush on him in seventh grade. Of course, so had most of the girls in my class.

He smirked. "Right, well, actually it's Alex now."

It was my turn to say, "I'm sorry?"

"I haven't gone by Xander since I joined the academy. I've been—"

"If you two are done *flirting*..." Amber dug her fists into the sides of her waist. "Can we get back to my dad? You know, the one who was hit by a car and killed last week?"

My eyes darted to the cement path in front of me, humiliated for more reasons than I could count. Thankfully, Xander—er, Alex—came to the rescue.

"I'm so sorry. And what was your dad's name?"

Amber crossed her arms. "Dan. Daniel Montrose. You're the officer who investigated, so you should know all about it, right?"

"I wrote up the report on the accident, yes." He bowed his head and shook it. "I'm so sorry about you losing your dad." Alex truly did sound sorry.

I took a deep breath, steeled myself, and joined the conversation. "So there was no investigation?"

Alex turned to me. I remembered those expressive emerald eyes. The girls in seventh grade used to joke about wishing on a two-leaf clover. "Well, yes. A team was brought to the scene when I'd discovered the extent of the damage, but I'm afraid West Virginia has one of the highest accident rates in the country, and we only have a small police department. Being Friday the thirteenth, and a full moon to boot, that night was beyond crazy for us. I doubt they've gotten far on this investigation."

I pulled back, surprised. "So you didn't even look for the car that struck and killed a man?" Even though this clearly didn't fall under his personal job description, I couldn't help addressing the question directly at him.

Alex shifted uncomfortably. "It hasn't even been a week. I'm sure they've had a forensics team out there by now, and when they get a chance—"

"When they get a chance?" I had read and helped with enough of Cooper's novels to know that if a crime scene wasn't investigated immediately, it would be of no use. "They haven't apprehended any possible drivers yet?"

"Where would you suggest we start, Mrs. Beck?" he asked in what sounded like a rhetorical tone. "Should we drop our other serious and pressing cases to check every vehicle in Honeysuckle Grove for traces of tissue in the event that the culprit hasn't already wiped the front of his or her vehicle with a rag and some bleach?" His words seemed to reverberate in the quiet air around us, and again he turned to Amber and said, "I apologize for being so blunt."

"Not every vehicle," I interrupted. "Only the ones with the right paint color and height. Forensics should have been able to secure some traces and identify how high off the ground the car was that struck him." Alex did a double take at me, which only spurred me on to say more. "They should have searched the roadside for clues as to what had gotten Dan Montrose out of his vehicle way out there, and if there was any significance behind it." I studied him as I said this, wondering if he had discovered anything in this regard. I certainly wasn't about to spill everything we had found to this unhelpful cop, no matter how attractive he might be. I'd much sooner speak to his superior.

Alex—or Officer Martinez, as I was trying to train myself to think of him since we were now using formalities—stared at me with his mouth open, as though at a loss of what to say.

"So there's nothing you can do to find out what really happened to my dad?" Amber asked.

He sighed and looked back at Amber. "Have you spoken to your mom about this? I've gone over the details with her."

Amber pulled her arms tighter across her chest. "The details like the fact that he was hit at Mile Marker 18?" Officer Martinez started to nod, but Amber had more to say. "Or the fact that there were no black skid marks on the ground near there, so the driver clearly didn't even try to stop? Or the fact that my dad had no reason to be out of his car, out in the middle of nowhere, and for some reason had mud on his shoes?" She let out a loud humorless laugh and then added, "Oh, right. None of those things were in your report, were they?"

I hadn't been ready to share all of that, but in an instant, I decided this was probably better. Let Officer Martinez give us some explanation for these things.

He took a step back from us, and then actually stepped into the flower bed lining the cement walkway to get around us. "If your mother has concerns with the case, have her call the department and talk to Captain Corbett. I was only the first officer on scene. I'm afraid there's nothing I can do."

A second later, Officer Martinez had raced up the path and disappeared into the police headquarters, not looking back once.

If that was one of Honeysuckle Grove's finest who we had to depend on to keep us safe, we were in big trouble.

Chapter Seven

MY PLAN TO HELP Amber find closure had backfired in a big way. As I pulled up to the curb down the road from her family's mansion, not only did she not want to get out of the Jeep, she was now convinced her father had been murdered and the entire police force of Honeysuckle Grove was trying to cover it up.

"Yes, there are a few things that don't add up, but that doesn't mean this was intentional," I told her, despite my own strong reservations. The fact that Dan Montrose had been out of his car at a specific mile marker, along a significant highway, kept tingling my Spidey Senses. It likely had something to do with my binge reading of Cooper Beck novels over the last eight months, I kept telling myself. However, Amber continually raising my suspicions aloud didn't exactly help.

"It doesn't mean it wasn't," she retorted.

"Listen, if you're concerned, I think all you can do is talk to your mom about it." She heaved out a labored sigh, expressing how much good she thought that might do. When she still continued to sit there, for so long I actually did consider the environmental unfriendliness of the Jeep, I added, "Let me give you my phone number. If you think of anything else I can do to help, let me know."

This seemed to satisfy her, and she pulled out her phone so I could rattle off my number for her. A second later, I felt my phone vibrate in my pocket.

"There. You have mine now, too."

"Okay. Great." I wasn't sure I'd instigate contact with this fifteen-year-old I'd just met, but this seemed to satisfy her enough to get out of the vehicle. "Talk soon," I said before she shut the door, and I didn't even know why.

Twenty minutes later, I walked through my front door, and sure enough, Hunch was sitting back on his haunches exactly where I'd left him. The second I closed the door behind me, he launched forward and sniffed every inch of the now-brown sneakers I wore.

"Hey, buddy," I said as though we were BFFs. Staring at my feet and my cat, the realization hit that I was going to have to get a hold of Amber again after all if I ever wanted my own shoes back.

Hunch let out something between a mewl and a growl. I often wondered if my inherited cat thought he was a dog. He sniffed over every new smell that entered our house, he growled on a regular basis, and he loved to go for car rides—at least he used to when Cooper had been alive. Cooper would have been able to decipher the friendliness of the sound Hunch made now, but I didn't speak Ornery Cat well enough yet. Today, though, I suspected I had some news that might get him on my side.

"So interesting thing at the wake I attended today..." I kicked off the dirty sneakers and led the way toward the kitchen. I glanced back to see if he'd find my conversation topic more interesting than my dirty borrowed sneakers. Soon he moved into the hallway behind me and followed me all the way into the kitchen. I started with, "The guy who died..."

because the word "death" in any of its grammatical expansions would certainly gain Hunch's attention. "It seemed this Dan Montrose was up to some strange stuff before his death."

I topped off Hunch's cat kibble in the kitchen. He just sat there, again on his haunches, staring up at me as though he couldn't care less about eating at a time like this. He wanted more of my story.

Fair enough. I wasn't lying about the strangeness. I went to the fridge to retrieve some sausages and peppers to cook up for dinner. Maybe I'd make a soup.

As I chopped vegetables and simmered onions with sausage chunks, I relayed the entire day's events to Hunch. The more I spoke out loud to the cat, the more normal it became, and I suspected the audible talking would do us both some good.

"I can't get over the fact that his death happened right at Mile Marker 18 on a highway that he'd been known to mark significant details. There were also some initials carved into a tree there, like at the other notable mile markers, but they weren't fresh, so he clearly hadn't just gotten out of his vehicle on the night of Friday the thirteenth to carve them out." I recounted the details of the missing skid marks, the muddy shoes, the freshly dug hole, but then returned to those initials. "What or who is F.D.S.?" I asked my cat.

Hunch looked up at me with his usual deadpan stare.

"Well, you're not much help, are you?" I winked to show him I was kidding—not that he would have understood my words. He took the odd bite of food while I described Amber, her brother and his friend, her mother and their housekeeper, as well as the rest of the wake-goers, but mostly he just lay on the floor, head on his front paws, staring up at me.

As I described each one of the people I'd come across today, I purposely played up his or her motive for murder, or at least covering up a murder, the way Cooper used to do when plotting a new novel. The embellishment was for Hunch's benefit, but as I finished with that skinny lawyer—Terrence somebody or other?—I wondered if I was exaggerating any of it.

"I guess the truth is, there could have been a lot of people who had a motive to murder Dan Montrose. He didn't seem all that well-liked, even by his own kids." I spoke the thought as it came to me.

Murder, even more than *death*, sparked Hunch's interest, and a second later, I looked down to find him rubbing his multi-shaded gray body against my legs. He had never done that before—not once in the half dozen years I'd known him.

"We even went to the police," I told him. I appreciated his affection and, to be quite honest, would have done almost anything in my power to make it continue. "But the cop on the case didn't seem to have the slightest interest in helping us figure out exactly what happened to Dan Montrose." I sighed, inwardly berating myself again for how I'd lost my focus because of a seventh-grade crush. "It seems like the police barely took the time to investigate it. If only that blockhead of a cop would've been willing to look into it, maybe I'd be able to stop the whole thing from rattling around in my mind."

I'd hoped calling Xander—Alex—Martinez a "blockhead" out loud would help me reset my attitude toward him, but the word still rang out as false, at least to my own ears.

Hunch paused and stood stock still against my capris and bare calves. I didn't think I imagined his fur prickle tautly against my skin. He let out another mewl/growl, but this time I could read the unfriendliness in it.

"I know," I said. "I wish he would've helped, too."

But Hunch only let out another mewl/growl, this one sounding even angrier.

That's when it occurred to me that Cooper's detective-assistant cat somehow wanted *me* to do something about this. As if to make his point clearer, he pad-padded down the hall toward the entryway, paused on his haunches, and let out another mewl.

I missed his softness and warmth against my legs—pretty much the extent of physical touch I'd received in the last eight months. At least that was the excuse I gave myself for following. I hadn't even gotten to the cat in the middle of the hallway, though, when he picked himself up and moved along with heavy footfalls, as if *he* were the one dragging a little mouse toy in front of *me*.

Not that Hunch had ever had the patience for toys.

I found him perched beside my dirty sneakers. "Yeah, they're a mess, aren't they?" I asked. "I suppose I should clean them, huh?"

Now my response was all growl—not a single bit of mewling.

This didn't surprise me. Deep down, I knew why I'd been summoned toward the front door. I just didn't know what in heaven's name Hunch expected me to do about it.

As if he realized I'd need direction, he started sniffing around, not only near my borrowed sneakers, but he covered every inch of the entryway.

"You think I should go back out to the site of the incident and look around?" I asked.

Hunch sat back on his haunches. If a cat could smile in satisfaction, that's exactly what I would have called the look on his little whiskered face.

I couldn't believe I was letting a cat push me around. But truth be told, I couldn't get the whole thing off my mind anyway. I hadn't taken a very thorough look around while we were out there earlier for fear of feeding into Amber's unrest.

Maybe it was a waste of time to drive back out to the site of the incident, but time was one thing I didn't lack. Maybe it would be a waste of gas, too. Then again, I could take the Prius.

I could only hope the trip would put both mine and Hunch's minds at rest.

Chapter Eight

APPARENTLY GOING BACK TO the crash site wasn't as easy as walking out the door and jumping into my Prius. After putting my soup on hold on the stove, I pulled on the dirty borrowed sneakers, headed out the front door, turned to pull it shut behind me, and there was Hunch, nose nudged through the opening.

"Oh. You want to come?"

I swear he looked up at me like I was daft. And I must have been because a second later, I scooped up the cat and brought him along. After so much time spent alone over the last eight months, with Hunch and me most often keeping to ourselves, the little bit of camaraderie I'd enjoyed with him today was addictive.

I had to admit, after driving Cooper's Jeep for my last dozen outings, my Prius felt low and small, almost as if I were an insignificant particle of dust in the greater world. I kept trying to reassure myself of my environmental responsibility, but I still couldn't help regretting my car choice.

Hunch sat up straight on the passenger seat as though he were human—or at the very least, part hound—and I was tempted to put a seatbelt around him. I highly doubted he'd allow it, even if it would fit.

"You're not going to pee or anything, right?" I asked, even though he'd never once had an accident in Cooper's Jeep or anywhere else he shouldn't have.

He didn't even dignify my question with a glance. In fact, he turned to gaze out the passenger window.

I'd chosen the dirty borrowed sneakers, as I figured they couldn't get much worse if I decided to trek down near the swamp again. It was nearing sunset, though, and I definitely didn't want to find myself down there alone after dark. I had great doubts that Hunch could do anything to protect me from a killer on the loose or even my own klutziness on that steep incline.

As I drove, I reached over and popped open my glove compartment, checking for my emergency flashlight. I pulled it out and dropped it onto the passenger's seat beside Hunch, and he rested one paw on top to hold it in place. Caught up in my thoughts of my cat and flashlight and how fast the sun may go down, I wasn't paying any attention to the mile markers until, suddenly, I passed Mile Marker 27, and familiarity made me quickly swerve onto the shoulder and slam my brakes.

On instinct, I threw out a hand in front of Hunch, but with his enviable nervous system, he barely budged. I let out my breath, checked behind me on the empty highway, and then backed the Prius up to the mile marker.

"December 27th is Amber's birthday," I explained to Hunch as I reached for the door handle. "Apparently, her dad carved something here on a tree a few birthdays ago."

With that, I hopped out of the car and headed for the shoulder and the nearest tree to Mile Marker 27. Sure enough, it took no effort at all to find a carved heart with the initials

A.A.M. inside it. The carved letters looked at least as worn and dark as the ones at Mile Marker 18.

I looked back at the car. Hunch was propped up with his front paws against the passenger window, apparently waiting to hear what I'd found. I snapped a quick photo with my phone and then quick-stepped around my car to get in and tell him.

I was so immersed in my excited explanation to Hunch, as well as my curiosity about whether the carved letters looked to be in the same style once I had a chance to compare, I didn't immediately notice the other vehicle parked on the far side of the shoulder as I pulled up to Mile Marker 18. It was an early 2000's model Toyota with a dented back fender. Rust had formed around the dent. It appeared to be empty, but its presence sent eerie shivers through my stomach.

"Why is there another car parked out here at Mile Marker 18, one that has clearly been in an accident?"

Hunch didn't answer, of course, but it still made me feel less alone to ask the question aloud.

The damage was on the back of the car, not on the front where it would be if it had struck a person on an empty road, and the damage appeared to have happened months or even years ago, I reasoned to make myself feel better.

But I hadn't yet turned off my engine, and I wasn't sure I wanted to. As if Hunch knew this, he let out a low growl.

Lost in my decision-making, I jumped in my seat when a knock sounded at my window.

I looked first at Hunch, who appeared perfectly calm, still resting back on his haunches. Turning slowly, I looked out my own window.

Xander—er, Alex... Officer Martinez had somehow snuck up along the back of my car without me seeing him. He had been home to change since we last spoke and now wore a gray hoodie with a pair of snug jeans riding low on his hips. Without his police cap, his dark hair, while trimmed short, still held the little bit of curl that reminded me of seventh-grade

Xander. It almost had the effect of making me warm toward him.

Almost.

I lowered my window. "What are you doing here?" I asked in a forced monotone.

"The same thing as you, I imagine. Come and look at something," he told me, already walking away.

I sat there, staring after him for a long moment. First, trying to regulate my heart rate, and second, trying to get over what a jerk Xander Martinez had turned into. I wouldn't have expected it from the sweet boy I'd known in the seventh grade.

A sudden claw to my leg made me cry out. "Ow!"

Hunch held up his paw as though he had zero remorse and would happily do it again. At least it brought the added reminder of why we had come here: to look around for clues as to what had truly happened to Dan Montrose. And if Xander Martinez wanted to show me another clue, jerk or not, I should probably get out of the car.

I reached for the door handle and immediately heard something akin to a purr from the other side of the car. Maybe cats weren't so hard to read after all.

But as I turned to shut the door, Hunch was already outside, rubbing up against my leg.

"Oh, sweetie, you should wait in the car." I had barely reached down toward him when his growl started, only making more obvious how wrong my endearment toward him had sounded.

I sighed. When Hunch had first followed Cooper home, he'd been a cat that roamed freely, indoors and outdoors. In fact, my and Cooper's first house, just blocks from the university, used to have a little doggie door that the cat used. A few months into becoming cat owners, I showed Cooper an article about how cats lived up to twice as long if kept indoors. The very next day, he had nailed shut the doggie door. Hunch hadn't fought it too hard, as Cooper still took his laptop out on nice days and let Hunch hang out on his lap, and he took him along on car rides often, but since Cooper's death, I couldn't recall if Hunch had been out of the house even once.

Maybe that was why Hunch didn't like me.

Whatever the reason, Hunch wanted no part of being left in the car, and even though I worried about letting him roam outside, I also didn't mind the idea of having some company out here—company other than the brash Officer Martinez.

I walked toward where Officer Martinez—I was determined to refer to him formally from now on—crouched at the edge of the shoulder of the road, inspecting something. When Hunch and I moved closer, I asked, "So you finally decided this was worth investigating, I guess?"

He shrugged and looked up at me, and I swore for a second he looked like the sweet seventh-grade boy I'd once known. "I always wanted to look into it further. The captain told me to get down the road to another accident ASAP, and the investigative team was already here." He shrugged again. "I have to do what I'm told if I want to stay on the force."

"Except now?" I raised an eyebrow.

He shoved his hands into his hoodie pockets and stood. "I'm on my own time now. It just kept gnawing at me after I talked to you earlier."

You and me both, I thought but didn't say. "And so what have you found?" We were right beside the tree with the carved initials, but he had been crouching, so I wondered if he'd discovered something else.

He twisted his lips. "Not a lot to go on, huh?"

I stood there for a long moment, debating whether or not I should tell him about the hole Amber and I had found earlier, and about Dan Montrose's muddy shoes. He wasn't the friendliest or most helpful guy in the world, and he wasn't even here in any official capacity. Then again, he, at least, had some police training. What did I know about this stuff, beyond having helped Cooper with a little book research a handful of years ago?

Before I could make up my mind, Officer Martinez squatted again, but this time it definitely had nothing to do with the tree. "Here, kitty, kitty," he called.

Hunch had moved into the middle of the road and was feverishly sniffing the pavement. I looked in both directions. No cars were coming from either way, but I supposed it was a good idea to get him off the road just in case one appeared when we were distracted.

But before I could march over and pick him up, Officer Martinez told me, "They cleaned up the blood around there. I don't imagine the chemicals they used would be good for your cat."

Amber and I had been looking for black skid marks. We never would have noticed this slightly washed-out splotch of pavement. I was thankful, at least, that Officer Martinez was able to shed some light on the location of where Dan Montrose had been killed. Now that he'd pointed out, it would be easy to find again.

That's why Hunch seemed to be in a frenzy of sniffing. "Oh, you'll never get him back by calling him cutesy names," I said. Instead, I turned to the cat and said, "Hey, Hunch? Come and look at this clue over here."

Hunch paused but then padded over toward us. He sat back on his haunches and looked straight up at Officer Martinez. The cop looked at me with a strange expression, as though trying to ask me telepathically if we were really going to share our clues with the cat. I gave him one solid nod, and finally, he turned back to the slope right beyond the carved tree and pointed.

Hunch rounded my legs and busily sniffed around what looked like a skidded footprint a few feet into the trees and down the slope. I was surprised I hadn't seen it earlier. I thought this was the exact same path I'd traversed with Amber. Although, come to think of it, I'd been more concerned with catching up with Amber at the time. I moved closer and could make out the deep impression of a heel with a long strip of skidded fresh dirt below it.

Hunch sniffed at the outer rim of the print, which made me murmur a question toward him. "Is it the same as mine?" Hunch glanced at me, glanced briefly at my shoe, which I'd outstretched toward him, and then returned to sniffing. "Did someone else go down here?" I asked my cat rhetorically. The footprint, now that I looked closer, seemed to be wider than my small foot.

Officer Martinez, oblivious to my one-sided feline conversation, said, "It looks as though someone climbed down here, and recently."

"Is that right, Sherlock?" I mumbled.

Hunch moved farther down the steep hill, and while Alex stayed behind to snap a few photos of the footprint with his phone, I carefully climbed down after Hunch.

"Are you sure you should go in there?" he asked from behind me. "It looks pretty steep."

It did. And it was. I'd already traversed it once today, after all. Thankfully, these high-quality, never-been-worn sneakers had good grip on the bottom because when Hunch stopped only a few more steps down the bank, I was able to hold myself there to see what he'd found.

I could make out a tiny swatch of purple paper smashed into the dirt. It wasn't even two inches in length, but on that two inches, it appeared to have a loop of black—though not enough to even spell out one letter.

"It looks like a swatch of gift wrap," I observed.

Officer Martinez moved closer behind me. "Hmm, you might be right. Don't touch it though," he added unnecessarily. "And don't let your cat touch it, in case it's important." He snapped another couple of photos.

I laughed and raised an eyebrow. As if I had any say at all over what Hunch decided to do. "Why? Because a tiny piece of a wrapping paper is going to show us what really happened to Dan Montrose?" I shook my head, trying to ignore Cooper's voice in the back of my head citing how significant small clues could prove to be.

"And you're right," he went on, "the paper might be nothing. But I didn't see much else in the way of garbage on the roadside near here. If someone threw it out their window, wouldn't we have seen more traces of it near the road? It looks more to me like a piece of paper—perhaps gift wrap—that had gotten stuck on someone's shoe, probably the person who climbed down here, and as you so astutely pointed out, there's not much reason for a person to get out of his car way out here."

I wasn't sure if the astute comment was sarcastic, so I chose to ignore it. I figured I should probably mention that Amber and I had climbed down here earlier, especially when we found three more clear footprints that were so mashed into the mud they could have been either of ours.

I kept my mouth shut, leading the way to the swampy bottom where the hole Amber and I had found earlier...

Had been filled in.

"What on earth?" I stood, shaking my head, while Hunch crawled low to the ground in a renewed frenzy of sniffing. He also knew something was clearly wrong here.

"What?" Officer Martinez asked. "Are you seeing something I'm not?"

I heaved out a big breath. "Amber Montrose and I climbed down here earlier today. There had been mud on her dad's shoes when she got them back from the coroner and she wanted to know why. Not three hours ago, there had been an open hole here, with dirt piled to the side. Someone has been back recently to fill it in."

"Or to bury something," Officer Martinez said, snapping a few more photos. "I wonder if I could get Steve Reinhart out here to take a look."

"Who's Steve Reinhart?" I bent to get a closer look at the newly covered hole but was careful not to touch anything. Hunch was also making a wide arc around the fresh dirt. My smart investigative cat didn't need to be told about the importance of keeping a clean crime scene.

"He's a detective on the force—one I'm somewhat friendly with. He wasn't on the case last Friday night, and too bad he wasn't, because he wouldn't have missed all these bits of possible evidence we're finding."

"Are you sure the other team didn't find them?" I asked. I didn't think I imagined Alex avoiding my gaze and my question. I stood from the muddy earth to press him. "How do you know what the investigative team found?"

Now Alex definitely avoided my gaze, but at least he offered an answer. "I had a quick look at the file before I left the station today. Unfortunately, the detective in charge is not…" He trailed off, looking uncomfortable, like he didn't want to discredit anyone on the force.

But I couldn't help but ask. "Is not what? A good detective? The most astute? What?"

Alex shook his head. "He's been known to let things slip."

I furrowed my brow. "And so what did he let slip this time?"

Alex sighed and spread out his arms wide to the sides. "All of it. The hole you said you found, the bright paper, the footprints." He shook his head. "There wasn't even a note about the muddy shoes."

"You're kidding?" I said.

"I wasn't going to bother Steve until I came out here to see if anything truly didn't add up. But when your young friend—"

"Amber," I put in.

"When Amber mentioned her dad's muddy shoes, and then when I found no mention of them in the report, I had to at least look into it."

I took a deep breath and tried to let my frustration over this go. It was equally frustrating not being able to touch anything, not being able to dig in the dirt and see if someone had really buried something. "Do you really think someone would come back to bury something right at the site of the incident? Doesn't that seem odd to you?"

Officer Martinez shrugged. "I've heard of stranger things. Murderers leaving so-called calling cards and such."

"So that's what we're talking about here? Murder?"

Hunch let out a low mewl. I'd forgotten all about him. He sat on his haunches, licking his muddy paws.

"I didn't say that," Officer Martinez said, clearly backtracking. "And you know I'm not here in any official capacity, right? I'd appreciate it if you didn't go down to the station and mention I was out here digging around."

I squinted at him. "You'd get into trouble for that?"

What kind of a careless police department oversaw this town, anyway? Or was it a sneaky, underhanded police department? I crossed my arms and thought about this. I'd quickly taken the police's word on the details of Cooper's accident, the same as Helen Montrose probably had with the information about her husband, but now I had to question if that had been such a smart idea.

"The captain specifically told me this was an open and shut case. He told me to sign off on it that night and I did. There's protocol..." Even Officer Martinez sounded as though this wasn't a very strong argument.

"Even if there was a possible murder committed? The captain can't mean that. Or if he does, it seems to me like there's something suspicious going on at the police department. Am I wrong?"

Officer Martinez shook his head and looked down at his hands. "No, it just...it's probably not even about this case. It's about Captain Corbett's biases. He likes who he likes in the department, he hates who he hates. In my case, it has to do with my dad."

"Your dad?" I squinted.

"Two years ago, he was on the force and got on the captain's bad side. I mean, my dad has transferred out of town since then, but Corbett still likes to call the shots with me. I can never question him. He knows I want to work my way up to detective, and he's always putting roadblocks in the way of that. It's why I barely spent fifteen minutes at the scene last Friday. Just long enough for the investigative team to arrive."

"What? I don't understand. You have to be able to do something, to tell somebody. What about this detective friend of yours?"

Officer Martinez locked his leafy green eyes onto mine, and suddenly, he was Xander again. Or maybe Alex suited him even more. "I'd encourage you to go into the station and report what you've found to the captain, I really would. I'd just...please don't mention my name. I could get in a lot of trouble for this. But besides that, believe me, if you really want to get to the bottom of this, it's better that you don't." In this moment, he didn't look at all like the brash police officer I'd spoken to earlier today. He looked like a puppy who had been kicked. "And I *will* talk to Detective Reinhart about what we've found. I'll do everything I can on my end."

He pulled a flashlight from his pocket and shone it around the filled-in hole. I hadn't realized how dark it was getting. "So someone was out here just to fill in the empty hole," he surmised. "Why would they bother?"

I pressed my lips together and thought this over while Hunch took to sniffing around the dirt once more, as if he were the detective and we were simply his lackeys. "I wonder if Amber told anyone what we found earlier. I know I didn't."

I looked at Alex, hoping I could trust him. I was pretty sure I could. "I told her if she was still worried, she should tell her mom."

Alex nodded. "Well, maybe that should be your first stop then." I looked at him in confusion. "If Amber has been in contact with anyone about this, or if someone may have even overheard her talking, well...Let me put it more plainly: If perhaps she's been loose-lipped with her discoveries around someone who could have intentionally killed Dan Montrose, I think you should check in on Amber as soon as possible."

Chapter Nine

I DIDN'T THINK I should show up at the Montrose mansion in my muddy state, after having muddied my second pair of capris today, so I headed home first, took a quick shower, and then started with a text to Amber.

~I wanted to come by and get my shoes. You around?~

I was certain not to add anything incriminating in case Alex had been correct and Amber was somehow now connected to a murderer. Only a second later, she returned my text, which put my mind at ease, at least a little.

~Yup. What about a cooking lesson? Or was that all talk?~

Hmm. I'd forgotten about my offer to teach her to cook. But that might give me the perfect excuse to talk to her alone.

~I'm up for it. You want to ask your mom if it's ok to come to my place? I can pick you up and drive you home after.~

Less than thirty seconds later, she texted back.

~Yup s'all good. Meet you at the corner.~

I doubted enough time had passed that she had actually asked permission, but at the same time, I was eager to get her out of there and probe her with a few questions.

Hunch seemed to know he wouldn't be coming along on the short car ride to pick up Amber. He'd been meticulously licking every inch of his fur since we walked in the door and he didn't stop now.

"Be back in fifteen," I told him on my way out, to which he responded by flipping a hind leg over his head to give himself a full bath.

Sure enough, Amber stood at the corner where I'd dropped her off earlier, my shoes in one of her hands and my clean casserole dish in the other.

"Thanks," I said when she passed it over. "I wasn't expecting the dish back so soon."

I wondered if it was Amber or their housekeeper, Lupe, who'd had the forethought to put the casserole into another dish and clean this one.

But then Amber told me, "Yeah, I had another helping and then I dropped it off at my brother's room. Danny and Cade inhaled the rest in about two seconds, so I figured I might as well return the dish."

I felt a wash of pride come over me as I turned the corner of Amber's street. When I had worked in restaurants, the chefs always received the praise, certainly not the prep cooks. Cooper had loved my cooking, but it had been a long time since I'd gotten any sort of compliment.

To cover for my flushed cheeks, I asked, "Your mom said it was okay to come to my place?" I still had my doubts. She didn't even know me.

Amber shrugged. "She didn't see my note from earlier, so I just left the same one."

"And your mom won't think it's strange that you've gone to see the neighbor's dog after dark?" I probed.

Amber laughed. "I doubt Mom would think it was strange if I went to the neighbor's house at three a.m. You know, as long as I was dressed appropriately and had some makeup on."

I thought back to how perfectly Helen Montrose's makeup had been applied, how perfectly put together she looked at her husband's wake, while her sister Beth had black mascara streaks under her eyes from crying.

"So then if you left the same note, you must not have told your mom what we found earlier? Where we went?" I pulled into my driveway and turned to her, but she looked back at me with one extremely raised eyebrow. "No?" I pushed. I needed an answer.

"Obviously." She let out a huff of a laugh. "She would have killed me. She would have killed *you*."

It seemed strange how easily Amber joked about her mom killing one of us under the circumstances. Or at least I hoped it was a joke.

She followed me up the steps to my front door and inside. We had barely stepped over the threshold when she dropped to her knees and squealed like a little kid. "Oooh, you have a kitty!"

Hunch had little patience for the "kitty" moniker, and he also had sharp claws and little tolerance for people touching him when it wasn't his idea, so as she moved toward him, I started to say, "Oh, Hunch isn't the friendliest of cats..." But I trailed off when, seconds later, Amber scooped him up into her arms and he nuzzled up to her neck. He was also *purring*.

"Well. He obviously likes you," I stated the obvious, trying not to feel the sting of his rejection toward me.

Come to think of it, one time almost two years ago, Cooper's dad came to visit. Cooper's mom had died after a long battle with cancer not long before that, and I recalled Hunch having the same reaction to Cooper's dad. He'd sat in his lap purring all afternoon.

Maybe I hadn't given Hunch enough credit. Maybe he was more than the novelist's ideal companion.

I led the way to the kitchen. "I should have asked on the way what you wanted to cook. I went grocery shopping yesterday..."—*and the two days before that*, I added silently—"but depending on what you want to make, we might need more supplies."

Amber followed me, Hunch still purring in her arms. She sniffed the air. "I was going to say we should make that same casserole, but whatever else you've got going on here smells pretty great, too."

I shrugged. "Just soup, but if you're hungry...?"

Amber placed Hunch down beside his food dish and nodded emphatically. Hadn't she just eaten my casserole for the second time today? But I served her up a bowl just the same. I also served myself some. I had left it to simmer as soon as I got home but hadn't actually felt hungry by the time it was ready. Maybe I could eat now that I had some company. It had worked earlier today in Amber's bedroom.

I sat across from her at the small, round kitchen table with my own bowl—a table I hadn't sat at in over eight months. Why eat in a kitchen by yourself when you could eat with your favorite TV characters?

"So you didn't tell anyone where we went today?" I wasn't sure if I should tell her that I'd been back out there with Alex, or that the hole had been filled in. She probably didn't need to hear anything that would feed her suspicions about her dad's death.

She took a slurp before answering. "Well, I told Danny, but he didn't care."

My spoon stilled in place. "You told your brother? What did he say?"

I thought back to how relieved Danny Jr. had been about not having to go to college and about the freedom he now felt about pursuing mechanics. I didn't think it was enough reason to kill his own father, but then again, I wasn't an angry teenager. At least not anymore.

Amber shrugged and continued eating. "He thinks I'm stupid for worrying about it since we can't bring Dad back from the dead or anything."

I took a small bite, mostly so I could keep an even voice. "And do you think your brother would want your dad back? If he could have him?" I kept my eyes on my soup, but then looked up when I sensed Amber's brooding silence. Again with the extremely raised eyebrow.

"Of course," she said finally. She placed her spoon down. "What are you saying?"

I waved a casual hand and took another bite, trying to erase the tension as well as the questions of why Danny Jr. had started going by his middle name and why he would tell his best friend about his relief to have his dad out of the picture. "I'm not saying anything. Just wondering if anyone could have overheard your conversation with Danny?"

Thankfully, Amber returned to her soup, unbothered. "Doubt it. I mean, if Cade was still there, he might have heard since we were right outside Danny's room. Come to think of it, Cade probably was still there because he came into the kitchen when I was washing your casserole dish."

Danny's voice came back to me. *My dad's dead, like you wanted.*

I nodded to Amber and made my voice as casual as possible. "Did you tell Danny about the hole we found down the bank?"

Amber shrugged. "Yeah, but he just thinks I go looking for trouble. He figured it was a dog or coyote or something that dug the hole."

It was possible, but would a coyote return to fill in his hole? I snapped my mouth shut before I could say this out loud, reminding myself I didn't want to share that part with Amber, at least not yet. Instead, I tried another tactic. "Did Cade know your dad very well?"

This made her snicker, and she showed me her empty bowl in request for more. I started to stand to get her some, but before I could, she was already up and across the room, helping herself. "Dad hated Cade. Kept telling Danny he should get some friends with some aspirations."

Odd, considering Cade had been the one surprised that Danny had no intention of going to college. But I decided not to mention that conversation either. "Do you happen to know Cade's last name?" I asked, again with forced casualness, but not much seemed to get by Amber.

"Why?" She dropped down into the chair across from me again with a fresh bowl of soup, looking me right in the eye.

I took a bite, stalling. Then another. Finally, I shrugged. "I was just thinking of going back to the cops, talking to the captain there, and if there's anyone who had anything against your dad, well, I thought maybe I should mention it."

Silence took over the room.

"If you don't want me to mention him, I won't," I said, even though I wasn't completely sure I meant it. Cade seemed to be the most likely suspect here of wanting Dan Montrose dead, at least if his son could be believed. And he also seemed to be suspect of overhearing about the hole out at Mile Marker 18. Then again, would Cade have had time to hear about the hole, drive out there to fill it in before Alex and I returned, and then get back to the house before Amber left? Perhaps just enough time.

I gnawed at my lip in disappointment as I wondered how close Alex and I might have been to catching Cade in the act.

Finally, Amber answered with a shrug. "I guess you might as well tell the cops anything that could be important, then hopefully they'll at least get off their butts and look into this. His last name is Peeters, with a double E."

I committed the name to memory and nodded. "Anyone else you think I should mention? Anyone who really disliked your dad or whom your dad disliked?"

Amber let out a humorless laugh. "How long have you got? Half the people at the wake probably thought Dad was greedy and corrupt and figured he needed to be taught a lesson. He called the cops or the city on neighbors almost weekly. He joked about defending people who had money, regardless of their guilt. He talked down to almost everyone. Half the lawyers at that backbiting firm would have done almost anything to clear the way to move up in the ranks."

"Anything? As in murder?" I asked.

Amber shrugged one shoulder, not offering a yes or a no.

"There was one lawyer at the wake named Terrence something?" I asked, hoping I at least had the first name correct.

Her forehead buckled. "Terrence Lane was there? I can't believe he'd show his face at our house again."

Terrence Lane sounded right. "What do you mean? Why wouldn't he?"

Amber shook her head. "Yeah, I'd definitely mention him to the cops. He's a real climber, has been trying to push anyone out of his way to make partner for as long as I've known him. Terrence was at that dinner party two weeks ago. I never stay for those things if I can help it, but my parents always wanted me to at least make an appearance. I remember I'd come down the stairs right when Dad had turned and knocked a drink out of Terrence's hand. I guess he'd been bringing it over for my dad, who'd already had one too many."

Amber looked up like she was picturing the whole scene, and I wondered how hard it must be for her to think of one of her dad's last moments like this. "After he hit the drink out of Terrence's hand, and Lupe rushed over to clean it up, he turned to Terrence, pointed a finger right in his face, and said, 'Stop following me around like some kind of mutt. We need smart lawyers at the firm, not sniveling idiots that are too principled to choose between a winner and a loser.'" Amber's eyes widened to demonstrate how awful the scene had been. "This was in front of everyone—every single lawyer and legal assistant at the firm. Then he added, 'You'll never make partner as long as I'm at the firm.' Terrence went beet red and then walked straight out our front door."

I made shorthand notes about the dinner party, already thinking about how I might be able to call into the firm and get someone else to corroborate the story. Terrence had seemed like he'd been looking for the person who had killed Dan Montrose at the wake, but perhaps that was only to cover up his own guilt.

"He had more motive than anybody, if you ask me." But Amber continued on, listing several other names of lawyers at the firm who had a grumbly attitude toward her dad at best, and she repeated each of their names and spelled them out so I could make a list. She went on to name extended family members who had never liked Dan and may have been after the Montrose fortune. I couldn't see how they'd think they'd have any right to it, but I made notes of their names all the same.

I would add her mother and brother's names to my list after Amber left. I couldn't shake my questions about Helen Montrose's unusual cheeriness at her husband's wake or the way his son had spoken so callously about his dad's death. I thought they at least warranted looking into, even if she didn't.

Amber didn't end up with anything in the way of a cooking lesson, but when I drove her home, I promised we'd get together again soon.

And hopefully by then, I'd have something more to explain the oddities surrounding her father's death.

Chapter Ten

APPARENTLY, IT TOOK A lot of convincing with just a touch of panic to get an appointment to meet with a police captain.

After nearly an hour on the phone the next morning, I'd finally tapped the long-suffering tendencies of the police department's receptionist. In the end, I'd had to stretch the truth and tell her that it wasn't a specific case I was concerned about, but rather a couple of officers and their incompetence. She had wanted the officers' names, but I insisted I would only give those to Captain Corbett directly.

I strode into the station just before eleven, cutting it closer than I would have liked. Hunch hadn't wanted to listen to reason when I told him animals were not allowed in police stations. I had practically heard him arguing aloud, "But what about police dogs, Mallory? What about them, huh?"

And so I'd argued along right back at him about how police dogs went through special training (to which I'd received some extremely raised eye whiskers) and how "each dog is assigned to a specific officer, and do you have a specific officer who would vouch for your presence because don't forget we're leaving Alex Martinez out of this."

In the end, I'd had to race out the door and pull it shut before he could follow me.

The police station reception was plastered with warnings of how to behave, wanted posters, and a bulletin board with a flyer advertising an upcoming police barbecue. The same receptionist who had dealt with us yesterday again greeted me with what I suspected was a suppressed eye roll. I felt somewhat smug as I told her, "I have an appointment with Police Captain Corbett at eleven a.m."

She looked me up and down, clearly less than impressed. Because of the summery weather, I'd chosen a coral dress for the day, complete with a matching headband, but under the receptionist's gaze, it suddenly felt unprofessional. I glanced down at the receptionist's nametag, which read "Hilary."

Hilary the receptionist made me wait fifteen minutes in the small, sterile waiting room. I considered texting Amber to let her know my whereabouts, but then decided I'd see if I could get some positive news to relay first.

"Miss..." Hilary looked down at her notes as though she couldn't quite remember the name of the sole person waiting for an appointment. "...Beck? Captain Corbett will see you now."

The receptionist spun on her heel and marched down a hallway. I guess I was expected to follow?

I jumped to my feet, suddenly concerned that this receptionist intended for me to miss my appointment after she lost me within the bowels of the police station. That wasn't going to happen if I had anything to say about it.

Hilary let out a loud sigh when I finally caught up to her outside an open office door. "Captain Corbett, your eleven o'clock appointment is here. A Miss Mallory Beck."

"Mrs.," I said, not because I cared about the distinction, but only because I felt the need to correct her about something.

Hilary didn't dignify my correction with any kind of response, and instead turned and quick-stepped away. I couldn't believe her rudeness. Then again, I guess it seemed as though I'd gone over her head after she wouldn't book me in to see Officer Martinez yesterday. I only hoped she didn't recall the specific officer or the specific case I had been asking after when Amber and I had been at her desk. I was going to do my best to keep Alex out of this.

"Come in. Have a seat," Captain Corbett said, motioning to a chair across from where he sat behind a large mahogany desk.

He wore a very decorated-looking black long-sleeve police uniform with a gold badge on his left breast pocket attached to several other gold pins with chains. There were also gold stripes and stars on patches along his sleeve. I didn't know what any of them meant, only that he must be capable. Alex had some sort of personal problem with this man, or at least his dad had, but in only a second, my hope grew that once given all the facts, this man would surely be able to help. He had a bushy gray mustache that matched the gray hair remaining on the sides of his balding head and clearly wasn't new to police work.

"I understand you have a complaint about someone within the department?"

I sat up straight on the edge of my chair, choosing my words carefully. "Well, not exactly, no. It is, however, about one of the cases your department recently investigated, and I have reason to believe there was foul play involved."

Captain Corbett furrowed his brow and flipped through a few pages on a legal notepad as though he might find the case in question right there in his notes. He picked up a pair of black glasses and perched them onto the bridge of his nose and then looked over them at me.

"Foul play? Is that right?" He didn't leave me time to answer, and I was glad. The question didn't quite sound rhetorical, exactly, but more like he was jockeying for position in this conversation. "And which case are we talking about here, ma'am?" His voice had a twang that sounded more Texan than West Virginian.

"It's the Dan Montrose case. You see, I drove out to where the car struck him, and I found it interesting that he got out of his car so far outside of town where there seemed to be no reason to, and I understand his car was operating just fine, and when I looked around more closely—"

"Helen Montrose said there might be a few of y'all comin' down here and tryin' to stir up some kind of a story." As Captain Corbett cut me off, he leaned back in his seat and put his hands behind his head in an obvious power position.

I pulled back in disbelief. "Sir, I'm not trying to stir up anything. I'm simply a concerned citizen."

"Right." He drew out the word as if to highlight the falseness in it. "And so you have no vested interest in this family or their commodities?"

I shook my head. "Absolutely not. I didn't even know any of them until—"

At this, he actually laughed. "Oh, I see. And so this is simply a good Samaritan effort is it, Ms..." He looked down at his notes to find my last name, and I felt in no hurry to provide it to him.

The gall! No wonder Alex had such an awful time working under this man. If Alex's dad had transferred out of town to find a new boss, I wondered why Alex hadn't followed suit. Then again, one thing I remembered about my seventh grade in Honeysuckle Grove was that everyone else was in a hurry to grow up and get out of this small town. Not me. I had loved Honeysuckle Grove more than any of the other places my dad had moved us to. And Alex had loved it, too. Said he would retire here. I remembered that.

"...Beck." Captain Corbett snapped his fingers as if he deserved some kind of a medal for suddenly finding my name on his messy, paperwork-covered desk. "Hang on, isn't there some mystery writer in town by that name?"

"That was my late husband," I said through gritted teeth. I did not like his tone.

"This ain't one o' your husband's stories, Mrs. Beck. You think you're the first one who's come in here demanding we draw out an investigation or dish out some sort of dirt to go into someone's article?" He laughed again. "Why don't y'all tell me exactly what kind of vested interest you have in this case, Ms. Beck, and I'll be certain to pass it along to Dan Montrose's grieving widow."

Grieving? I wondered if he'd actually met Helen Montrose face to face, or perhaps the woman had put on more of a show of mourning at the police station than she had at her own husband's wake. In fact, this whole line of questioning—which Captain Corbett had somehow turned around on *me*—made me wonder if Helen Montrose and Captain Corbett had made some kind of a private agreement regarding the investigation of her husband's death. I hadn't wanted to think of Helen Montrose as a serious suspect in the killing of her own husband, but maybe I shouldn't be so quick to dismiss her.

"Mrs. Montrose will know you by name, I assume?" Captain Corbett pressed. The more he spoke, the more intimidating he became, as though he could sense that I truly was sticking my nose where it didn't belong, and he was going to keep pushing until I admitted it.

"You can tell her it was a concerned citizen," I told him, standing.

The longer I stayed here, the angrier I became, not just at Captain Corbett, but at Helen Montrose, Danny Jr., and his friend Cade Peeters. With Terrence Lane and with anyone who'd had odd behavior at the wake or motive to kill, and most definitely at whoever had actually driven their car into Dan Montrose.

I reached for the door. "Thank you for your time, Captain."

I definitely couldn't thank him for his help, now could I?

If Amber was right about her father being murdered, and everything I'd found at the scene of his death indicated she was, it was clearly up to me to figure out who was responsible.

Chapter Eleven

THAT NIGHT, AMBER, ALEX, and I stood in my kitchen as I described my meeting with Captain Corbett in detail. This was our Dream Team, it seemed. I'd lured Amber over under the guise of another cooking lesson, and I'd had to look Alex up in Honeysuckle Grove's online phone directory to get a hold of him, but I didn't think I'd be able to figure this out without either of them.

"I can't say I'm surprised." Alex leaned back against the counter and shook his head when I got to the end about Captain Corbett threatening to go back to Mrs. Montrose with my name. "Corbett likes to throw his weight around, but I was still hoping that having the information come from an outsider might do some good."

"My mom likes to throw her weight around, too." Amber bent to pet Hunch, who had been rubbing affectionately against her legs since she arrived. "She's also overly concerned about anybody being into our business. She probably told the police captain to deflect any focus from this case as quickly and quietly as possible, and I'll bet she said it in a way that came close to sounding like a threat."

I peeked at my crab cakes in the oven. They weren't quite done. Strangely enough, the buzz of having all these unanswered questions gave me the same type of energy as a bustling kitchen once had. I hadn't stopped cooking since I'd gotten home at lunchtime. "I don't see Captain Corbett simply sitting back and taking a threat from random townsfolk."

To this, both Alex and Amber laughed. I raised my eyebrows at both of them until Amber explained.

"Oh, believe me, my parents have never been random townsfolk. They practically own the mayor of this town. Why do you think we have a downtown street named after us?"

I blinked once and then again. "Wait, Montrose Avenue is named after *your* family?"

Both Alex and Amber chuckled as if this were old news.

"Okay, well, I wish I would have known that." My mind raced with this new information. I grabbed the bag of flour from one of the bottom cupboards and plunked it onto the counter. "So all we have to do is talk our way into another appointment with Corbett. This one is for you," I told Amber. I wasn't sure what to make with the flour, but finally having a promising next step filled my hands with nervous energy again. I wanted to knead.

Amber stood, and Hunch resumed offering his full affection against her legs. "Wish it were that easy. My parents have clout. Or I guess only my mom does now. Nobody will listen to me, least of all the police captain." She turned to Alex. "You'd know that better than anyone." She turned to me to explain. "I'd been sleeping over at my friend Shayla's house, but I came home early the next morning as soon as Shayla's mom told me what had happened." She turned back to Alex. "You wouldn't even let me in the same room when you gave my mom the details of the accident."

"That's because your mom insisted." Alex took one of my kitchen chairs, flipped it around, and sat backward on it. He was in casual clothes again, jeans with a green plaid button-down that matched his eyes.

"See?" Amber said, arms splayed open.

"She has a point." Alex helped himself to one of the snickerdoodles I'd made earlier this afternoon. "So, listen, I convinced Steve Reinhart to drive out and take a look at the scene. He had the same concerns, seeing the footprints and the hole that had been filled in, and called Corbett to get permission to get a forensics team back out there. Corbett told him Detective Bradley would handle it."

My eyes widened with hope, but the look on Alex's face made that hope deflate. "Why? What's wrong with Detective Bradley?"

Alex shook his head, his gaze on my small table. "There are dozens of unsolved hit-and-run accidents on the books, and Bradley's the laziest guy on the force. I don't even know how he made detective, but somehow, he seems to be one of Corbett's favorites. In other words, if Corbett wanted this case swept under the carpet, written off as a simple hit-and-run with no motive or suspicious circumstances, Bradley's the guy to do it."

I rolled out my dough. I'd unthinkingly grabbed some yeast from the fridge, measured some warm water, and added sugar and salt all while Alex had been talking. I started mixing and slamming the dough down onto the counter, which immediately helped clear my head. "Okay, fine. So where do we start if it's up to us to find out the truth?"

"We haven't found any solid evidence that there's foul play involved, and I can't—" Alex started, but I had no patience for him trying to back out of this.

"Listen, you don't know everything, okay?" I glanced at Amber for the go-ahead. She gave me one single nod, so I turned back to Alex. "That wasn't just any highway that Dan Montrose died on. He had carved his and Helen's initials at Mile Marker 5 to commemorate their wedding day. He'd carved Amber's initials at a specific mile marker to commemorate her birthday." I paused for effect, and then added, "And we found FDS carved on the tree right behind Mile Marker 18."

I turned to Amber, letting that new information sit with Alex. "You said your dad had a lot of enemies, but who would have wanted him out of the picture the most?"

Amber shrugged. She took a seat across from Alex and helped herself to her own cookie. "Lawyers, relatives, neighbors. Like I said, it could have been anybody."

I blew a breath up toward my bangs, even though they were pulled back with my coral headband. "No one person in particular? No burning hatred?" I already had a couple of names in mind: Cade Peeters and Terrence Lane. But I wanted her to corroborate them.

She twisted her lips, thinking about it, but the passing seconds only served to frustrate me.

"Okay, let's start with this: Why might your mom want to curtail an investigation? I know she wanted to keep it quiet, but was that only because of local gossip?"

Amber's head snapped toward me. "I don't know, but she didn't kill my dad if that's what you're saying." I replayed my words, and it did sound as though that's what I had insinuated. I opened my mouth to backtrack, but Amber went on. "Believe me, it's not because she's some kind of saint. Mom suggested firing different people at the firm like she was throwing out yesterday's newspaper, but trust me, she isn't the type to do any kind of dirty work herself."

Huh. That did sound like Helen Montrose, at least the little I knew of her.

"Speaking of dirty, you took all your dad's shoes and clothes when they came back from the coroner. I'm curious as to why?"

Amber shrugged and reached for another cookie. "Mom actually left them for Lupe to clean, and then they were going to get given to a thrift store. I don't know what I thought I'd do with them, but I just couldn't handle that idea, not so soon at least, so I brought them to my room. I still haven't been able to bring myself to clean them." She looked down at the floor as though this embarrassed her.

"Well, if you hadn't mentioned the mud, we might not have found that hole yesterday," I told her.

Alex interrupted before I could think of anything else to say to make her feel better. "And was anything else on his person? Did anything else get returned from the coroner with his clothes, like a cell phone, perhaps?"

"Isn't that something the police should know?" I asked and regretted it the second it left my mouth. Alex's eyes flitted away. Now I'd made them both feel bad about their actions. "Never mind," I added quickly. "I get it. Bradley took over the case. Of course all the clothing and belongings would have ended up with the coroner, but why wouldn't they be in any kind of report? I can't believe that the whole coroner's department is that lazy."

Alex shook his head. "I can't get access to the coroner's report. Normally, it's copied to our main police report, but for some reason, it didn't make it to Detective Bradley's paperwork. There's simply a note that says, 'See coroner's report.' But there was one note from forensics."

I stared at him, waiting.

"Nothing major. Just that it had been a low-riding dark blue vehicle that had struck Dan Montrose. There were traces found at the scene." My hope started to rise again but was squashed only a second later when he added, "But not nearly as much detail as I would expect. There's no exact shade of blue, no metallic content, not even any idea of where the paint color was lifted from—on Dan Montrose's body or somewhere else at the scene. There would be thousands of vehicles that match that description in Honeysuckle Grove alone, not to mention the outlying towns."

I separated my dough, at a loss for where to go from here, with baking or with the case, but Amber's mind was still on other aspects.

"His cell phone came back to us, too," Amber said. Both Alex and I stared at her until she went on. "Mom's pretty much a technophobe, so I think she gave it to Danny to reformat it. I'm not sure where it went. Danny probably still has it."

I looked to Alex, wondering if he could do anything to find cell phone records—without his boss finding out. But I couldn't ask that of him.

I turned back to Amber. "Yesterday afternoon at your house, I overheard a conversation between your brother and Cade. I got the impression Danny wasn't planning to go to college, you know, now that your dad's not around to argue it." I figured this was no time for secrets, and I needed to get all the information out on the table. "I know Cade hated your dad, but how did Danny get along with him?" I kept my voice gentle, so this wouldn't be mistaken for an accusation again.

Amber shifted uncomfortably. It took her several long seconds to answer, but I waited her out. "Lately not great. He hasn't been listening to either of my parents much lately, and that night of their dinner party with the firm? Danny was supposed to make an appearance, too, but he ended up staying out all night with Cade. When Danny came in the next morning, Dad tore a strip off him and said he wasn't to spend another minute with Cade Peeters."

"But Cade was there at the wake. Your mom didn't care about that?"

Amber shrugged. "I don't think she didn't *care*, it's just...she just hasn't been able to concentrate on anything besides keeping up a strong front and the funeral arrangements."

I had to wonder if that was what made her appear so cheery and put together at the wake—staying singularly focused. "And when did your brother start calling himself Seth?"

"About a year ago." She looked down at the table. "I don't think it meant anything."

"You don't think changing his name away from that of his dad signaled anything serious?" I wanted to slap myself. *Again with the thinly disguised accusations, Mallory!* But thankfully Alex intercepted.

"In my experience, a name change isn't always about distancing yourself from someone or reinventing yourself as a different person."

I supposed Alex would know about name changes. If he'd wanted to distance himself from his dad's reputation within the police force, I would've thought he would have changed his last name.

"For me," he went on to explain, "it had to do with another guy in the academy, also named Zander—with a Z. Still, it got confusing, and he didn't have a great chance of graduating." Alex shrugged. "So often I think it can be for a really simple reason."

Amber crossed her arms over her chest, not letting my accusing suggestion go. "My brother didn't kill my dad either," she said, still clearly upset with my wording. But the waver to her voice told me she wasn't a hundred percent sure. Still, how difficult would such a thing be to process?

"Nobody's saying he did," I told her gently. "But don't you think Danny's anger at his dad warrants asking him a few questions?"

She furrowed her brow and looked down at Hunch, who still wound himself back and forth and around her legs.

She didn't answer, and so I added, "You don't even have to be a part of any questioning if you don't want to be, Amber. In fact, it's probably safer if you aren't."

Her head snapped up, and her furrowed brow deepened, but now it looked more determined than confused. "If my family members could have had any part in my dad's death, I need to know about it. No one's leaving me out of any more conversations." She balled her fists on the table.

"Fair enough," I told her. "So let's figure out how and where we can talk to your brother."

Chapter Twelve

THE NEXT MORNING, I drove the Prius down the mile-long driveway to Honeysuckle Grove's only golf course with Amber and Hunch in my passenger seat.

"You're sure he's here this early?" I asked.

Amber shrugged. "Well, no. But Lupe told me he left the house wearing a polo shirt." She scratched Hunch under his chin, which he seemed to appreciate. "Danny is very good at dressing for occasions."

"And a person has to dress up to go golfing?" I had no idea. I'd never been golfing and had only dressed in a pair of white capris with a peach cardigan this morning, as it promised to be another warm sunny day. Even less dressy, Amber wore jean cut-offs and a purple hoodie that read: BONJOUR. G'DAY. ALOHA.

"Nah. But most people do, and if you want to go into the club, you have to."

I nodded and parked several spaces away from the nearest car, a Jaguar. Looking over the parking lot, I took in the other half dozen cars. Ever since Alex had mentioned the traces of blue paint found at the scene of Dan Montrose's death, I hadn't been able to stop thinking about Danny Jr.'s vehicle—a blue Corvette I'd seen with my own eyes.

But the Corvette was nowhere in sight.

"How would he have gotten here?" I asked Amber. I didn't want to feed into her suspicions of her brother until I had questioned him, but I had to suck in a breath when she shrugged and pointed to a maroon sedan. "He brought your dad's car?"

She shrugged again and nodded as if this was no big deal.

In an effort to regain my even keel voice, I turned and looked at Hunch. "Now I told you, you can't come along for this part, right?"

Hunch seemed smarter than the average cat, but I still could never tell how much he understood when it came to the English language. It hadn't hit seventy degrees yet this morning, but I cracked my window open, along with Amber's, and a second later, Hunch stretched on Amber's lap and then happily leaped into the backseat.

At least that was one problem off my mind.

"Danny doesn't get out of bed early unless he's either forced to for school or golfing."

I nodded. "Who do you think he's here with?"

She shrugged. "Who knows. Probably met up with some other guys from the club. He used to golf with Dad, back when they got along better, but lately, he goes at least once a week and doesn't talk about who he plays with."

"And you're sure Cade won't be here with him?" I'd asked this by text earlier and she'd only answered with a quick "NO", but now she expanded on her answer.

"I'm pretty sure Cade can't afford a membership. He definitely wouldn't be accepted into the country club."

The way she said it, so bluntly, seemed to add motive to Cade as a suspect. We got out of the car, and Hunch remained in the backseat, licking his paws.

"Have you golfed much?" I asked Amber.

She led the way across the parking lot, toward the Pro Shop. "Not really my thing. But Dad made me go once or twice a year."

"Can't we just go out onto the course and find your brother?" I asked, hesitating as we closed in on the Pro Shop. My skin itched at the thought of too many people knowing about us investigating Dan Montrose's death. If it got back to Helen Montrose that I was putting suspicious thoughts into her daughter's head, or back to the police captain about me sticking my nose into somewhere it didn't belong, it could mean trouble.

But Amber only laughed, unbothered by the concept. "You want to search an eighteen-hole golf course, be my guest." She held out a hand toward the miles of green grass that started at the edge of the pavement, and I understood her point.

Thankfully, she knew something about the procedures of a golf course, which was more than I could say for myself. It was just after eight a.m. on a Thursday, and even with the few cars scattered in the lot, the Pro Shop was empty, save for one man folding shirts at a display table. Amber marched straight for the counter, and the man stopped his folding and met her on the other side.

"What can I help you with?" The man's nametag read SCOTT. He wore white pants and a pink collared golf shirt so bright it made me wonder if it was Breast Cancer Awareness Month.

"I'm looking for my brother, Danny Montrose. Can I find out his tee time?"

Scott rattled his mouse to bring his computer screen to life and then scrolled through a short list of names. "I don't see a Danny— Oh, wait, there's a Seth Montrose. Could it be listed under a relative's name?"

Amber rolled her eyes at me and then turned back to Scott. "Yeah, that's them." As Scott ran his finger across the screen, Amber murmured to me, "My multiple personality brother."

"Not too many around yet. He was one of the first out at 7:16. You should find him around the sixth or seventh hole by now."

"Gotcha," Amber said, holding up a hand in thanks.

"Thank you," I called as I followed her out the door.

Even though Amber had only golfed a handful of times in her life, she thankfully seemed to know the course well enough to navigate to the sixth hole without a map. Two men were teeing off, but Danny wasn't either of them, so we continued on to the seventh hole. Even knowing where to look, it was still a lot of walking, and I heaved out a heavy breath when we stopped on the green and stared around at the vast empty hillside around us.

"It's usually busier in the summer," Amber said. "Although Dad and I never came this early. I guess it makes sense why he might be ahead."

We moved around a small grove of trees toward the eighth hole and saw Danny, just setting up his ball on a tee. He was alone.

"This couldn't have worked out better," I murmured quietly to Amber, but her forehead creased in confusion.

"Hey, Danny?" she called out before he could take his first shot.

His shoulders slumped at his name, but he didn't immediately look over to us. In fact, he stared off in the opposite direction. "Can't I go anywhere to get some time to myself?" he said to the far side of the golf course.

Now I felt bad. My solitude had meant everything to me in the early days after Cooper's death. No matter how angry Danny had been with his dad, he would still be grieving and probably needed some time on his own, too.

Amber clearly didn't clue into this line of thinking. She marched straight for her brother, crossed her arms, and said, "My friend here has some questions, and Lupe told us we could find you here."

Finally, Danny turned toward us, but his gaze stayed on the sky as he shook his head and murmured, "Stupid Lupe." He finally looked at his sister. "What does your *friend* want to ask me about?"

I was pretty sure Danny must own a sweatshirt about sarcasm as well. Or he should.

"I just think...we both do..." I motioned to Amber and myself. "That something's fishy about your dad's death. Maybe it's nothing, but we want to make sure." I carefully watched Danny for his reaction, but he only took in a big breath and let it out on a loud sigh, as though we had already exhausted him.

"Is this about that stupid hole Amber found? Has she gotten you all riled up about that, too?"

It seemed he wasn't going to be overly helpful, but because he also hadn't shut down the conversation so far, I forged ahead. "It's not only that. Where were you the night that your dad died?" I dropped my tone softer, again thinking about his possibly conflicting feelings.

Danny reached for his upright golf bag as though searching for a different club. At first, I thought he might ignore my question, ignore me, but then he said, "I was home. Playing video games with Cade."

"All evening?"

One solid nod.

"Just you and Cade?"

Another single nod.

"And I understand your mom was out at a charity event. Did she call you with the news?"

Danny shifted his shoulders as though the question made him uncomfortable. But at least he answered it. "Nah, she came through the door just after ten, crying and freaking out. I told Cade he should probably go out the back way. He did, and then I came down to find out what was wrong."

"And your mom told you what had happened?" I confirmed.

Danny let out a humorless laugh. "I guess you could call it that. Took quite a while to decipher her words." Danny slipped the club he was holding back into his bag and grabbed another. He turned it in his hands but didn't make any effort to resume playing.

"Your mom seemed much more composed by the time I saw her at the wake," I observed. Sure, it had been almost a week later, but I had still been a walking zombie a week after Cooper's death.

Danny scratched at his red-brown hair. The short ends turned up as though they would be curly like Amber's if he let it grow. His cheeks darkened, and he looked at his feet. I got the impression he didn't want to answer this, but I waited him out.

Finally, he looked me straight in the eye, and angry words erupted from his mouth. "Maybe she had a good reason to act like she had it all together. Maybe she's a good actress. I heard she held it together for a few hours at the wake, kept muttering something about the will and its stupid stipulations all morning. Who knows with her. We're just kids, right? No one ever tells us anything." An edge of bitterness leaked out in his voice, and he seemed as though he was pointedly avoiding Amber's eyes, but I wasn't sure how to pry about his feelings toward his parents.

Instead, I decided on a different line of questioning. "So Cade was there playing video games with you all night? The night of your dad's death? He would vouch for you?"

Danny's face darkened, and he gripped his golf club so hard his knuckles whitened around it. "What are you here for? What are you implying?" He looked between me and Amber, and thankfully, Amber stepped in.

"She's not accusing you of anything, Danny. I told her you're not behind this—that's why we came to you for help. She just wants to confirm your alibi before we start prying into other people's business, so no one can point the finger back at you." It was a good tact—to put this all under the guise of protecting him. Maybe Amber truly meant it that way. If I were being honest, I still wasn't completely convinced.

And then, to make matters worse, Danny shrugged and said, "Alibi? Pfft. Well, if you're looking for an alibi, truth is, I probably don't have one. Cade went out for snacks sometime after eight. I told him we had plenty downstairs, but he wanted some spicy Cheetos or something. I can't remember. Anyway, he ended up being gone for almost an hour. Came home just before Mom did."

An hour to get snacks seemed like a long time. "Did he have a car?" Before Danny could even answer, I added, "What kind and color is it?"

Danny screwed up his face, likely because I was pushing the blame toward his best friend now, but Amber answered me.

"He drives this bright green Ford Fiesta. He calls it his frog. The thing is so old and ugly, he always parks it down the block."

Old, ugly, and noticeable. Danny wasn't supposed to be hanging out with Cade, and yet there was an eyesore of a car clearly stating that he was on the very night of his dad's death. That had to mean something. But also, did his car's paint color clear Cade of suspicion?

"Could Cade have borrowed your Corvette to go to the store?" I blurted the thought the second it came to me.

But it only caused Danny to laugh, and this time, it sounded like something truly was funny. "Sure, if he'd wanted to replace the carburetor, weld the exhaust leaks, and slap the tires back on first." He laughed again.

I looked between Danny and Amber. "The Corvette doesn't run?" I hated to admit it, but relief washed over me at this new bit of information.

Danny jutted out his chin. "It will."

Amber openly rolled her eyes in a way that made me think this was an ongoing argument in the Montrose household.

"And your mom was driving her Tesla that night?" I asked, just to check, even though I couldn't in my wildest dreams imagine the hated friend, Cade Peeters, being permitted to drive that beautiful car.

Danny squinted. "Of course. Why?"

I looked at Amber, but her gaze remained squarely on her brother. "What about Lupe? Wasn't she there that night? Couldn't she confirm you were there?" Like a dog with a bone, Amber wasn't going to let this point go until she could find an alibi for her brother.

She had already told me she had been sleeping over at a friend's house the night her dad died, but Lupe usually worked until whenever her son, Nando, got off work and came back to pick her up. Most days she was there until ten or eleven at night.

Danny's hands relaxed around the golf club, and his eyes roamed back and forth over a patch of grass in front of him. "Oh. Yeah. I guess Lupe was somewhere in the house. She came to try and help calm Mom down after she came in freaking out, but I waved her away. I didn't see her again after that."

That made me feel better. At least Lupe would be able to verify he had been there. If Cade had left for over an hour, only to come back with a bag of spicy Cheetos, and if he overheard the conversation about the hole by mile marker 18, green car or not, he was beginning to look like the most likely suspect. He had motive—as Danny had clearly said, "My dad's dead, like you wanted."

He had opportunity, as he was gone from the Montrose house and alone when it happened. All I had to figure out was the means. Was it definitely a blue car that had struck Dan Montrose? Or could the traces of paint have been there from another accident? Could Cade Peeters have used someone else's car to strike down the man?

I had made some notes the night before, and I glanced at the notepad from my purse to go over them. "One more thing," I said to Danny, but just then the two men who had been playing their own game a couple of holes behind Danny appeared from around the grove of trees.

"Oh," one of them said, stopping in surprise. "Sorry."

Danny let out a low growl under his breath and glared at his sister. When he turned back to the men, his voice took on forced pleasantness. "Nope, my fault. Go ahead and play through. I'm going to be a few minutes, apparently." The last word was loaded with his frustration, even if it still sounded pleasant toward the strangers on the surface. His mom wasn't the only one who could act.

We followed Danny behind a nearby bench.

"What's this one more thing?" he gritted out, making his frustrations more than clear.

"When your dad's stuff came back from the coroner, I heard his cell phone went to you, to wipe it?"

He glanced at Amber so quickly I almost missed it. "I, uh, didn't get around to that yet."

"No? Can we have a look at it?"

Another glance at Amber. "Look, I don't think you want to, okay? I don't think *she* wants to." He motioned to his sister.

I had seen Amber get choked up more than once while talking about her dad, but no matter how much she didn't know about him, I suspected she already understood he wasn't a glowing example of humanity. She needed her unanswered questions put to rest.

She cleared this up for Danny. "You think I don't know what Dad was like? What, was he screwing someone out of their money again?" She slapped her cheeks and made an O with her mouth. "Oh, I'm so surprised. Or, what? He was sleeping around?"

"He was sleeping around with Auntie Beth!" Danny hissed, interrupting her.

They both stood there, stunned—Amber at the news, and Danny that he'd said it out loud. Clearly, Danny hadn't meant for it to come out so bluntly. Thankfully, the second gentleman who was playing through had taken his shot and the men had already started to wander away after their golf balls, leaving us alone for the moment.

"I...you're wrong..." Amber looked like someone had just kicked her dog-friend Tinkerbell. "I don't think she—"

Danny nodded. "I thought I was wrong for a long time, too. I *hoped* I was wrong, but ever since Mom gave me his phone and I hacked his password, I know I'm right."

Amber's gaze flitted back and forth over Danny's face. Slowly, it looked as though she was starting to believe him. Soon I would have two very upset teenagers on my hands.

"I understand if this is a sensitive topic for Amber, for both of you," I said. "But as someone who can see this whole thing objectively, would you be willing to let me see what's on the phone?"

I hadn't yet decided what I'd do if he said no, if they both said no, because I just knew there would be something on that phone that would lead us to the truth.

Danny let out a low humorless laugh. "Have at 'er. I turned off the security." He motioned to his sister. "Amber can do what she wants, but trust me on this one..." He met her eyes head-on. "You won't be able to unsee any of it."

Chapter Thirteen

I STOPPED DOWN THE road from the Montrose mansion so Amber could run in and retrieve her dad's phone from Danny's bedroom. He'd told her where to find it and had given her one last warning that she might not want to see the explicit texts between her dad and her aunt.

I had only gotten her to agree to let me look at it *with* her so far, but I'd continue working on convincing her to let me give her an overview.

From my vantage point, I could see the edge of the large Montrose property and all of its manicured shrubbery. A young gardener was busy clipping some of the slightly overgrown branches. I debated ducking down in my seat, but the gardener seemed oblivious to me.

The more I watched him, the more familiarity struck, though. I pulled out my phone and snapped a photo when I caught his profile. Zooming in, I could see I was right. It was the housekeeper's son—Nando, was it? I wondered if he regularly helped with the gardening around the mansion or if he was doing it as a favor to Helen Montrose—who Amber mentioned had taken a liking to the boy and his boundless manners.

The more I gazed at the zoomed-in photo, the more I could see an edge to the young teen. There was anger behind his clenched jaw, and so I suspected it was his mother who had roped him into helping with the gardening and not the matron of the house who appreciated him so much.

In my distraction, a dark blue Tesla sailed by me, snatching my attention. On instinct, I ducked. Helen Montrose drove a dark blue Tesla!

Soon, the Tesla turned into the Montrose driveway and moved out of sight. I let out my breath. It hadn't occurred to me until after Amber and I had left the golf course, but the new information we'd gotten about Dan Montrose's affair with Amber's Auntie Beth seemed to make her mom into the number one suspect. She owned a dark blue Tesla, a low-riding vehicle that matched the police report. Then again, I looked along the curb of the street and at least a half-dozen dark blue vehicles were in view just in this one block.

I shook my head, reminding myself she also had a strong motive. If Dan Montrose was having an affair with Helen's sister, and there was some sort of stipulation in the will that made her put on an act as though everything was fine when clearly it wasn't, it only shed more suspicion on her. It was strange. I'd only met Amber two days ago, and yet my heart ached for her as though I'd known her for years.

My heart stuttered when Amber hopped back into the passenger seat of the Prius and dropped a cell phone into the middle console. She had taken the route through the neighbor's yard and seemed to have missed seeing either her mother or Lupe's son, who had now disappeared out of sight somewhere in the Montrose's large yard. Hunch, who had been patiently waiting on the floor of the passenger side, hopped up onto her lap.

"You'd never know it, but that's not the friendliest cat in the world."

Hunch, as if on cue, immediately started purring like a race car, and Amber looked over at me with a raised eyebrow.

To get the subject off my traitorous cat, I asked, "Does Lupe's son always do your gardening?" I motioned my chin toward the yard, even though I couldn't see him at the moment.

"Nando?" She scrunched up her face, but soon after, it flattened to something more understanding. "I suppose it makes sense. Dad didn't like Nando, called him 'that Mexican kid' whenever he was hanging around. Mom loves him, though, and Lupe probably wants the help." She shrugged.

"Alex is meeting us at my place on his lunch break," I told her as I swung a U-turn toward my place. "Apparently, the case file had some new information, and he has something to tell us. I hope that means it's being investigated further."

"Huh. I wonder if it's about Cade."

"Cade?"

Amber nodded. "While I was inside, I called Danny to get Cade's email address. Danny thought I was just confirming his alibi so he gave it to me right away. But I figured if Cade's our most likely suspect, I could set up a time to meet him somewhere. I'll keep my phone recording in my pocket in case I can get him to admit to anything."

"Hmm. Let's talk to Alex more about that first." I tried to make my voice sound even and unconcerned, even as alarm bells went off all over the place inside my head. I was not about to let a fifteen-year-old go fishing for information from a possible killer by herself—even if I no longer thought of him as the most likely suspect.

Then again, letting her go home and sleep in the same house with her mother each night could just as easily involve danger.

I shook my head as I pulled into my driveway. I suspected my overactive, murder-mystery-binging mind inhibited my ability to think straight sometimes. Killing your husband in a heated rage over an affair was different than killing your own daughter.

Alex had already parked along the curb. Hopefully, he would put some perspective on the whole thing.

He met us at my front door. He wore his police uniform again and took off his hat as he met up with us. I braced myself for him to act brash like he had last time he'd been in uniform, but when he opened his mouth and motioned to Hunch, still in Amber's arms, his voice actually seemed playful. "You bring your cat everywhere you go?"

"Not if I can help it," I grumbled. I opened the door wide to let them go in ahead. Hunch jumped out of Amber's arms and trotted toward his food dish in the kitchen, human affection all but forgotten.

"I understand you found your dad's phone?" Alex asked Amber.

"Uh-huh."

"Was it wiped?"

Amber shook her head. "Danny said he hadn't gotten around to it. We haven't looked at it yet, though."

Tension edged her voice, so I redirected the conversation. "You said you found something of interest in the file, Alex? Did Captain Corbett decide it deserved another look?" We all headed for the kitchen.

"It might be nothing," Alex said. He and Amber took their usual seats at the table, and it seemed my fingers itched to cook again. I was making far too much food for one person these days. Far too much for all three of us, in fact. Even still, I pulled roasted chicken, bacon, Swiss cheese, and alfalfa sprouts from the fridge and then headed for my breadbox for a fresh loaf. I'd whip up a nice chipotle mayo to round it out. Alex added, "But there was a note tacked on today, indicating Captain Corbett would be in attendance at the will reading."

"Will reading?" I asked as I carved off six slices of pumpernickel. "I thought those only happened in the movies."

There hadn't been a public will reading for Cooper or his mom, nor for my grandmother a few years ago. In Cooper's case, I had been the one to dig out the will and deliver it to the law office, and as the sole beneficiary, it was dealt with in just one afternoon between me and my lawyer. We'd never seen Cooper's mom's will, and in my grandmother's case, I had received a copy in the mail, followed by some jewelry a month or so later. But what did I know about how these things worked? Maybe will readings were a popular event for the rich.

Alex went on to explain. "They don't have them often, no, but if any contention is expected, or if specific stipulations apply, then sometimes they do. What's truly odd, though, is that the police captain would be required at one."

My mind stuck on *specific stipulations*. "Danny said there were some stipulations in the will. He didn't sound like he knew what they were, though. How can we find out?"

"That's why I wanted to meet you at lunch today." Alex opened the sealed container from the middle of my table and helped himself to a pecan tart. Amber followed suit. I kept working on their sandwiches, keeping my motherly comments about ruining their appetites to myself. "The will reading is this afternoon," he said around a mouthful of tart.

"Today? Really? Where?"

"At this estate lawyer's office." Alex pulled a folded paper from his pocket and laid it onto the table. "I don't know how easy it would be to eavesdrop on this thing, but I figure if the police are invited, it could be a fairly large gathering."

"Well, obviously, I can't go," Amber said, but she didn't look as deflated by this realization as I expected. Her next words explained why. "While you're busy, I'll send that email to Cade, see if I can get somewhere on investigating him."

I turned to Alex. "Amber thinks her brother's friend Cade Peeters had something to do with the accident. We found out he and Danny were playing video games the night of Dan Montrose's death, but Cade needlessly went out for an hour to buy some snacks." Alex's eyebrows knit together, so he was definitely listening, but I enunciated the next part, as I wanted him to hear this section the most. "Amber thinks she should set up a meeting and dig for information from Cade, using her phone as a recording device."

Amber nodded, eagerness written all over her face and clearly not noticing my concern.

After a long minute of thinking this over, Alex said to Amber, "Hmm, a phone probably isn't the best recording equipment, especially with someone who might be nervous."

I widened my eyes at Alex. Was he seriously *encouraging* Amber in this?

He turned to me next. "You should probably get ready for the will reading. It starts in half an hour."

I looked down at myself. I'd worn capris and a cardigan out to the golf course, which I suspected wasn't exactly will-reading attire, but I couldn't leave the room while Alex egged Amber on about questioning Cade on her own.

But then he turned back to her and said, "How about I nose around the station and try and find a wire for you to wear? It just might take me a day or two." Amber lit up at this suggestion. "Go on," he said to me. "We'll be fine." As I started to leave the room, Alex threw me a quick wink. *Ahhh, he was buying time.* "Now why don't we figure out what's on your dad's phone."

He picked it up from the table as I left the room, and I hated to admit it, but I was glad they were figuring that part out without me. The more I thought about it, the more I knew Amber would absolutely not have let me keep anything on that phone from her. But I also didn't particularly want to be around when she set eyes on any incriminating messages from her Auntie Beth for the first time.

Funny, when Beth had shown Cooper and me houses around Honeysuckle Grove, I'd known she was single, but I could never have imagined her as someone's mistress. Even now, I felt like I needed to see some incriminating evidence to believe it.

Then again, I supposed it would be hard to believe that kind of deceit of most people. That was why they called them *secret* affairs. I only hoped Alex would clue into the fact that this made Helen Montrose our prime suspect for the murder of her husband without me having to outright say it. Or perhaps he already understood this. He had encouraged me to go sit in on this will reading, after all.

I pulled on a pair of pantyhose and made certain of no extra pairs riding along on the outside of my navy skirt before pulling that on, wondering what Helen Montrose would select for her wardrobe at a will reading. Would she be composed like at the wake, or a crying mess like Danny had described her?

Ten minutes later, I straightened my navy blazer on the most boring and drab outfit I owned as I walked back down the stairs. The key was to be unnoticeable, I reminded myself.

When I walked into the kitchen, my wardrobe became a distant memory. Amber held a crumpled Kleenex in her hand, and her eyes were red. Alex continued to scroll through Dan Montrose's cell phone, but it seemed Amber had seen enough.

"Was it true? What Danny said?" I asked softly. I didn't want to spell it out again.

Amber nodded into her lap.

Alex spoke in an equally soft voice. "I've skimmed through all of his texts from the last couple of weeks and a few of his emails, and the messages between him and Beth are the only things to raise any red flags so far. But Amber's going to let me keep the phone to go over it a little closer."

"Does this mean my mom killed him?" Amber burst out, and a new flood of tears erupted from her eyes.

I took a chair beside her and slid my arm around her. "No, sweetie, it doesn't mean that. We don't even know if your mom knew about what had been going on between your dad and her sister, and we haven't even asked her any questions yet." I had to admit I still had my strong suspicions that she knew very well what her husband had been up to, and therefore had a pretty strong motive, but I wanted to deliver that news to Amber in bite-size pieces.

Alex cleared his throat. "I have some work to do this afternoon around the grounds of the library, but I thought Amber could come along if she's up for it. Maybe she can confirm a few alibis from there." He raised his eyebrows in question toward Amber, and my knotted stomach loosened in gratefulness for him in that moment. I wondered if he had a little girl of his own at home. I also wondered if he was actually allowed to bring a teen civilian along to his job. Whatever the case, he sure knew how to brighten her up.

Once decided, we all stood and headed for the door.

"Should we meet back here after five?" Alex asked, again with the playful smirk. "It seems as though you've cooked up enough food to feed an army." They were both taking their sandwiches to go, but I no longer felt hungry. His smile flattened suddenly, and he added, "Oh, unless it's a problem with your husband?"

Alex looked around the entryway as though he might spot some of Cooper's shoes or coats lying around. It occurred to me in this moment that when I'd introduced myself as Mallory Beck at the police station. That came along with some assumptions.

But I still wasn't used to talking about it. "Oh. Um. No, it won't be a problem."

Thankfully, Amber rescued me from another difficult moment. "Come on, Officer Martinez." She opened the door for him. "I'll tell you all about it on the way."

I was grateful for that kid. In only two days of knowing her, she had brought a lot of good things into my world. I hoped I would be as much of a positive force in her life.

Or, at the very least, I hoped I could be a shoulder to cry on through some hard truths that might be on the horizon.

Twenty minutes later, I parked across town at the offices of Estate Lawyer Nelson Reed. The tall building housed at least two dozen businesses, but I easily located Mr. Reed's office on the wall directory near the elevator on the first floor. Several other people walked through the glass front doors and headed for the elevator, and when I stepped on and they pushed button 5, it seemed we all had the same destination.

Thankfully, I'd chosen well with my outfit. Most men wore dark suits, and the one woman on the elevator wore a black skirt and blazer similar to my navy one. I had added a matching wool fedora, and it seemed to do the trick of keeping people's interest away from my face.

When the elevator door opened, I blended with the crowd as they moved down the hallway toward office 518, but then they veered off suddenly at two wide-open doors.

They all headed inside a large boardroom with close to fifty seats, and I made a quick decision to follow. Perhaps large gatherings were held here instead of in the lawyer's actual office.

A dozen people were already seated, while others milled around talking. I spotted Helen Montrose right away—the sole person wearing a pink floral dress to this event. If she were a Jekyll and Hyde type, today was clearly one of her brighter Jekyll days.

She snapped her fingers high in the air and said, "Nando," loud enough that most people in the room looked her way. That's when I noticed Lupe and her son, Nando, at the perimeter of the room, offering up platters of cookies to guests.

Nando immediately grinned at Helen Montrose and wove his way over to her. She stood with a well-dressed couple I didn't recognize, and Nando seemed to know without being told why he had been summoned. He offered the cookie tray to the couple, and they both helped themselves to one.

Strange that Helen Montrose brought her own housekeeper and her son to a will reading. Wouldn't the law firm offer that sort of thing? Perhaps Mrs. Montrose simply liked to flaunt her wealth.

A lineup had formed near the coffee, so I decided against getting myself a cup. No need to put myself in a situation where someone might ask how I knew the deceased. Instead, I lingered just outside the doors and kept my eyes down on my phone.

Every couple of minutes, I peeked up from under the brim of my hat to take in more of the room and its occupants. Beth Dawson had arrived, but so far, I hadn't seen her anywhere near her sister. She didn't look as broken up today, and instead smiled and nodded as she greeted different folks around the room. Her somewhat glassy eyes and pasted-on smile made me wonder if she was medicated. I pulled my hat an inch lower, as she would be the most likely of the attendees to recognize me.

The only other familiar face was that of the lawyer from Dan Montrose's firm, Terrence Lane. In his same three-piece suit, he looked like a skinny giraffe, almost cartoon-like with his ultra long, thin legs and angular features. He moved through the room, talking to different attendees for only a few seconds each, but he had the air of someone on a mission.

As I took a step through the open doorway to follow Mr. Lane's progress around the room, out of my peripheral vision, I caught sight of a man in police uniform, striding down the hallway toward the boardroom.

Captain Corbett! Shoot, I had forgotten about him. I turned in the opposite direction to put my back to him and took quick steps back into the hallway.

By the time I turned back, a man in a pinstripe suit and glasses sat behind the table at the front of the room, flipping through a set of papers, and cleared his throat.

Most of the chairs in the room filled quickly with the lawyer's presence, and while a few open chairs remained near the front of the room, I would be far too obvious there. And, in fact, a second later, Captain Corbett helped himself to one of the front row seats. I wanted to sink into the floor or a wall to make myself invisible, but instead, my next best option was to inch my way behind one of the open doors. I took deep, steadying breaths as I moved, keeping one eye on all of the familiar people in the room to make sure they didn't look back at me.

A second later, I had made it to safety and let out a gust of air. Unfortunately, the lawyer in the pinstripe suit didn't have a terribly loud voice. I only made out bits and pieces as he announced the will reading and how it was being held at the request of Daniel Montrose. I'd have to ask Amber later why her dad might have requested a public will reading. I wondered if both he and his wife enjoyed flaunting their wealth—even after Mr. Montrose wasn't here to do it personally.

Then again, perhaps this would be his way of announcing his affair with Helen's sister.

Mr. Reed continued the spiel, asking that any contestations be made publicly today before submitting them formally in writing, and proof of stipulations was to be met today.

The more he spoke, the more I wondered if Dan Montrose had only suggested a public will reading for the drama of it.

The lawyer droned on, reading a lot of legalese from the actual will. I made notes on a small notepad from my purse, not sure how I'd make heads or tails of any of it. Maybe Alex could help me later, or I could meet with an independent lawyer. I only hoped I would understand enough to figure out what transpired during these proceedings.

Mr. Reed did most of the talking for at least half an hour. I tried not to tune out and kept popping candy from my purse to keep myself alert. He spoke of Dan's house, his vehicles, artwork, and personal belongings, all going to his wife, Helen Montrose.

"Any contestations?" Mr. Reed asked, to which there was no response.

Business holdings became more complicated, as Dan's law firm interest was assigned a value, which could be bought out among the partners. Several lawyers spoke up, arguing the amount, and I peered through the crack of the door to see if Terrence Lane added to the discussion.

He didn't. Then again, if he had been trying to make partner, I supposed he wouldn't have any kind of vested interest in Dan Montrose's holdings in the firm.

Mr. Reed knocked on his desk with a gavel. "If you would like to contest this point formally, you may proceed in writing. Until then, the value of Mrs. Montrose's assets in the firm stands."

Some grumbling throughout the room followed, and I made a note of the contention.

"If that's settled," Mr. Reed said, "let's move along."

He read several other points in the will, and almost every item seemed to be promised to Helen Montrose, so it confused me why all of these other people had gathered, if not simply for some kind of dramatic show. But soon smaller items cropped up, bequeathed to other people: An antique watch went to his son, Daniel Jr., a specific painting went to his brother, Ben Montrose, and a cabin at Cedar Lake went to Beth Dawson. Mr. Reed went on, and surprisingly, Helen Montrose did not contest this gift.

"The stipulation on cause of death," Mr. Reed announced. "In the case of suspicious cause of death or suicide, all allocations here within become null and void. In such a case, all properties named within shall go to the Clinton Foundation."

The Clinton Foundation? Huh. The Montrose Family wouldn't have struck me as Clinton supporters. But I clued back in when Mr. Reed spoke again.

"Do we have someone present who can verify this?"

"Yes, sir. Captain Corbett from the Honeysuckle Grove Police Department." Captain Corbett's voice boomed out much louder and more commanding than Mr. Reed's.

"And what has been declared the cause of death?" Mr. Reed asked.

"The death of Daniel Montrose was deemed an accident, without clear intent, by hit-and-run."

"Well, then," Mr. Reed said. "Thank you for your attendance, ladies and gentlemen. All points within the last will and testament of Daniel Montrose stand."

Immediately, a rush of activity erupted throughout the room. Seats shuffled on the floor, people grumbled to one another or chattered animatedly, and one person swept out into the hallway so quickly, I ducked into the tiny space behind the nearest door, so as not to look as though I had been lurking.

And good thing I did, as the person was Beth Dawson. I could only make out a small sliver of her, but she suddenly stopped within that small sliver of my vision only a foot from my hiding spot.

"I guess you'll leave us alone now," Helen Montrose's voice said, although I couldn't see her from behind the door. "Too bad you only got that stupid cottage. You obviously never meant much to Dan."

Beth Dawson let out a single huff of a laugh. "Dan knew I never wanted anything from him. If you want the cottage, you can have it. I just want Dan back!" Her words became louder at the end, as though she were physically chasing her sister.

But I could still make out the small swatch of her in front of me.

After a couple of seconds, I clued in that Helen had returned to the boardroom. Beth Dawson stood alone, watching her sister's retreat, and if I played it right...

I quickly slipped away from around the back of the door while Beth was still focused on the other direction. "Beth?" I said as though surprised to see her.

She turned, and her face was a contorted mess. Tears streaked her face, but she forced a smile upon seeing me. "Oh, Mallory, hi. What are you doing here?" She swiped a hand at her tears.

I passed her a tissue from my purse and motioned further down the hall. "Just meeting with Cooper's estate lawyer about some unfinished business. These things take forever to wrap up." It hadn't been true in Cooper's case, but Beth wouldn't know that.

"Unless you have boatloads of money," Beth murmured under her breath, but I heard her fine. I just didn't know what I was supposed to say in response to it. Thankfully, Beth shook her head and added, "I'm sorry. I didn't mean anything by that."

"Are you here for something to do with Dan Montrose's death?" I asked, all wide-eyed and innocent.

Beth's face immediately crumpled, and she swiped away more tears. She nodded until she could get her voice back. In that moment, I felt like I could confidently say that Beth Dawson had truly loved Dan Montrose. I wondered if that would make Amber feel better or worse about the whole situation.

Finally, she said, "Yes. It was his will reading. But I should really go."

I nodded and gave her a quick hug before letting her hurry down the hall and into the elevator. I remained in the middle of the wide hallway. Dark-suited people trickled out of the room and also headed toward the exit.

I could certainly use my ruse again—simply here to see another lawyer—but was there anything else I could accomplish here? Maybe I should just go.

Just then, Terrence Lane made his way out of the boardroom. His face looked twitchier than the last time I had encountered him at the Montrose mansion, and his fingers trembled as though he'd had too much caffeine.

He headed down the hall in the opposite direction of everyone else, toward the lawyer's offices, and as he moved farther in that direction, I saw my opportunity to converse with him privately.

I raced ahead, rooting in my purse for my notepad and pen, an idea suddenly coming to me. "Mr. Lane? Mr. Lane? Can I please have a minute of your time?"

Terrence Lane stopped in place and immediately started wringing his hands. "Yes, miss? What can I help you with?" Again, he had the double wink to his eye, and I had to remind myself it was a twitch. This man wasn't hitting on me.

"I'm Mallory Vandewalker," I said, in an instant deciding on my maiden name, "from the Honeysuckle Grove Herald." Everything I knew about journalists I had learned either from TV or from when I'd helped research Cooper's novels. Still, I forged ahead. "I was hoping to talk to you at the wake. Helen Montrose indicated you were investigating the vehicle involved in the hit-and-run accident of Dan Montrose. Can you comment on that?"

Terrence Lane became even more jittery, if that were possible. He glanced toward the boardroom, and his face took on a mask of indecision. "Helen Montrose told you that? She told you to speak to me?"

I doubted I'd get by with a bald-faced lie on this one. "She indicated you'd had some leads."

"I...um...I'm afraid I can't speak on that." He flicked his thumb against a fingernail.

"Even off the record?" I asked, folding up my notepad. "You see, I've been assigned to this story, and I feel it in my bones that there's something more to it, someone who should have come forward, but I'm afraid with everyone being so tight-lipped about it, I've found myself at a standstill."

Terrence's dark eyes flitted back and forth over mine. Close up, his angular cheekbones gave his face a sunken appearance, and each of his expressions was starkly different from the one before. I could tell how much he wanted to open his mouth and say more to me.

I tucked my notepad into my purse and put on my most trustworthy face. "I honestly won't report anything you tell me. I just really hoped not to go back to my boss and tell him I couldn't find anything to go on here. Can you give me any kind of a hint of where else to look?"

Another glance toward the boardroom, and then, to my surprise, Terrence Lane grabbed me by the arm and tugged me farther down the hall and around a corner. I quelled the yelp that wanted to come out of my mouth.

Terrence leaned in and told me in a rushed whisper, "You can't tell a soul I told you this. Not a soul," he repeated, to which I quickly nodded, "but I found out from the Montrose's mechanic, Mel Stanley, that one of the Montrose vehicles was brought to him the day after the accident." Terrence glanced toward the corner, but everything remained quiet at this end of the hallway. "Actually, he didn't tell me that, so you may not want to barrel in there asking questions. He wouldn't tell me anything, but I saw it scrawled on his desk planner."

"And what was the make of the vehicle? What was the color?" I asked, quickly thinking through every Montrose vehicle: the un-drivable Corvette, the dark blue Tesla, and the maroon car Dan had been driving. Then again, there had been a Ben Montrose mentioned at the reading.

Terrence shook his head. "Didn't say. It just said, 'MONTROSE FIX FRONT FENDER ASAP.'"

I nodded, searching for my next question, but Terrence didn't let me ask it.

"Find out which Montrose vehicle it was, and I think you'll find out who did this to Dan."

My mind swirled, but Terrence Lane raced away from me before I could ask any other questions.

Chapter Fourteen

BACK AT THE HOUSE, I pulled together a stir-fry while I waited for Alex and Amber to arrive. Chopping broccoli, carrots, and sweet white onions seemed to be a good way of funneling my energy. I had only just started simmering my ginger and garlic when a knock sounded at the door.

Sure enough, Amber and Alex stood on the stoop, and when I opened the door for them, they walked inside, already talking.

"All I'm saying is that it's not a very effective place to patrol," Amber was telling him. "You woulda caught way more speeders on Selkirk. It runs beside the highway, so everyone wants to go faster."

"Right. I'll keep that in mind in case Corbett one day says, 'Hey, Martinez, why don't you choose your own patrol route today?'"

They had the sort of easy bickering about them that made me think of a brother and sister, or a teasing uncle. I suspected Amber had been trying to rattle Alex's cage all afternoon.

They followed me to the kitchen, barely taking the time to say hello. When they got through the kitchen door, though, their bickering finally came to a halt.

"What smells so freaking good?" Amber didn't leave me time to answer. She followed me over to the counter to survey my assembly line of preparations. "And when did you say you were going to teach *me* how to make some of these recipes?"

I smirked and passed her my knife. "You want to slice up these water chestnuts?" I showed her the size I wanted, and without another word, she got to work.

It gave me a moment to catch up with Alex. As soon as I met him at the table, he stood from where he had already plunked down into his usual chair and placed a hand on my arm.

"Hey, I was sorry to hear about your husband," he said softly. "I didn't know."

My eyes flitted to a piece of floral art on the wall to keep them from watering. "Right. Yeah. Well, now you know."

Thankfully, he seemed to understand that I didn't much want to talk about Cooper, not when I'd already had such an emotionally taxing day. "I'm eager to hear about the will reading, but let me tell you what we came up with first."

I sat across from him, glad to have the focus on the Dan Montrose case.

"While I was patrolling, Little Miss Smarty Pants over there spent some time at the library checking up on her mom's alibi."

Amber grinned over her shoulder, and then went back to chopping. She carefully worked at the water chestnuts, trying to get them all exactly the same size. I could have told her not to be so concerned, but I had the feeling she, like me, enjoyed having something else to focus on.

"First, she emailed Cade." Alex must have caught my concerned look because he quickly elaborated. "We agreed she shouldn't arrange a meeting just yet, so instead she just asked him where he buys his spicy Cheetos. She told him she was in the mood for some and the grocery store was sold out. Then she called Honeysuckle Grove Parks and Trees Foundation, for which Helen Montrose had been attending a meeting the night of the accident," Alex told me. "She pretended to be an employee from the meeting hall where they had gathered and asked to double-check the exact meeting time, as well as setup and tear down for her records."

I raised my eyebrows in Amber's direction, but she didn't turn to see the praise. Alex went on. "I, myself, can vouch for Mrs. Montrose's presence at the hall an hour after the incident, as my partner and I had delivered the news personally. But Amber checked in with a few Instagram accounts of women she knew were on the board of the foundation with her mom. Their photos showed her on the stage all evening. To be sure, she messaged these women and heard back that her mother had been on the stage throughout the entirety of the meeting. So Helen Montrose could not have been the one to strike her husband with her car," he said, spelling it out for me.

I thought through everything I had learned that day, including what Terrence Lane had told me about the Montrose vehicle that had been repaired. "Do we know if she was driving her blue Tesla that night?"

"Doubt it," Amber said over her shoulder. "Usually Molly Taylor picks her up for all those board meetings."

"Can we find out for sure?" Alex asked. He had obviously caught on to my line of thinking. Because if she hadn't been driving the Tesla, we were back to suspecting Danny again. His only alibi was their housekeeper, Lupe, and we hadn't spoken with her yet.

Amber's voice suggested she was oblivious to our thoughts. "Sure. I'll message her when I'm done with this."

My mind was a rattled mess. I didn't want to think Danny, a boy of only seventeen, might be capable of purposefully killing his dad. I stood and headed for the counter, deciding to get the sauce simmering. Maybe that would help me think.

As soy sauce and hoisin began to fill the kitchen with new sweet and salty aromas, I took a deep breath and told Alex and Amber all about the will reading.

When I got to the part about the Cedar Lake cabin going to Beth Dawson, Amber's chopping—now onto yellow peppers—became louder and faster. "She used to go there with us when we were little," she said, bitterness leaking out in her voice.

I couldn't think of a single response that would make Amber feel any better about that, so I moved onto the next point. "And I found out about the will stipulation your brother had spoken about," I told them. "Apparently, if his death was a suicide or suspicious in any way, all allocations in the will would be void, and all of Dan Montrose's fortune would instead go to The Clinton Foundation. It's in my notes," I told Alex. I had left my notepad on the table for him to look at, but I couldn't stop thinking about this point, because the death certainly was suspicious. So who had the most reason to cover that up?

"The Clinton Foundation?" Amber stopped chopping completely. "Are you sure it said that? My parents hate Hillary Clinton. Especially Mom."

Alex confirmed the fact. When he found the clause that I'd hurriedly scribbled, he read it aloud.

"Huh." Amber resumed chopping. "It sounds like some kind of a slap in the face to me."

I dropped some rice noodles into my pot of boiling water, wondering what that meant. Had Dan Montrose *expected* some sort of foul play in his death? Then again, if he was having a serious affair with Helen's sister, I wondered if the stipulation had been a recent addition to the paperwork.

I went on to tell them about the altercation between Helen and Beth that I'd overheard, and then what I'd found out about the car repair from Terrence Lane.

"He was really jumpy, so I wasn't sure what to make of that."

Amber dumped her peppers into the pan of already simmering veggies and then waved a casual hand. "He's always like that. Mom's told him more than once that he should lay off the coffee, but he never listens to her. She doesn't sign his checks." Amber smirked. Clearly, she didn't seriously suspect Terrence of wrongdoing, and to be honest, neither did I. "But what he says is true. Mel Stanley is our mechanic. He's the only person Mom'll let work on her Tesla."

"So if your mom was definitely at that board meeting, picked up by Molly Taylor, and couldn't have been out wrecking her own car—which she would take in as an emergency repair the next day—who could have driven a blue Montrose car out by Mile Marker 18 that night?"

Even though I suspected I knew who—at this point, it had to be Danny Jr.—I waited for Amber to come to the same conclusion.

But she only shrugged, looking unbothered as she used my wooden spoon to stir the vegetables. "Danny's Corvette's up on blocks, Dad was driving his car, and Mom's Tesla would have been in the garage."

I nodded. "Right, but who could have been driving it, if not your mom? Could Cade have borrowed her vehicle from the garage?"

Amber let out a loud cackle of a laugh. "No way, Dad specifically told Danny that Cade wasn't allowed to use any of our cars. Ever." I watched as this all started to piece together in Amber's mind. A swallow traveled down her throat. "It coulda been Lupe, I guess," she said, but her words didn't sound terribly convincing.

"Could it have been?" I pressed.

"She doesn't borrow our cars often, but Mom's told her to take the Tesla a couple of times for an errand when Nando had Lupe's car." The more Amber spoke, the quieter she became. She knew we had to check up on Danny Jr.'s alibi next.

But then Alex placed my notepad down on the table and said, "Did it have to be a Montrose vehicle?" I furrowed my brow and started to nod, but he added, "Couldn't it have been a vehicle that the Montrose family simply paid to have repaired?"

That brought us back to implicating Helen Montrose in some part of her husband's murder or, at the very least, its cover-up.

Still, I hoped this thread of new possibility wouldn't fall apart the moment we pulled at it.

Chapter Fifteen

THE SUN HAD SET long ago. Amber and I organized a plan to spend the next morning questioning Lupe to see where that led us. Unfortunately, Alex had to be back on duty.

I wasn't crazy about the idea of Amber spending the night at home, but I hadn't come right out and said that. I'd asked her if she wanted to check with her mom if she could finish up a cooking lesson tonight and then stay over. I mentioned it under the guise that it just seemed easier than driving her home tonight only to meet back at her place in the morning. She'd texted her mom and simply received a response of: OK.

I wasn't sure what to make of that barely involved parenting but tried not to judge. The woman had just lost her husband, after all.

"Oh, and Cade emailed back," Amber said, still looking at her phone. "Says you can get spicy Cheetos anywhere, but he got some just last week at the little supermarket at the corner of 3rd and Hemlock."

"That's just down the hill from your house, right?" I asked.

Amber shrugged and twisted her mouth like the thought was distasteful. "Not really. It's all the way down in the flats. Plus, it's in an area where the lowlifes hang out. I suppose I shouldn't be surprised Cade went there."

"Why don't I look into the store first thing tomorrow," Alex said, standing from the table and heading for the front door. "I'll be done at five, so do we want to meet back here?" Alex opened the front door, but then turned back. "Or if you think you'll still be at Amber's place, maybe I should change into some casual clothes and meet you somewhere closer to there?"

"Here's fine," I told him, already excited about the prospect of making another dinner for more than just myself.

I followed him outside and took a few steps toward his patrol car. As he was about to step into the driver's side, he stopped and looked up at me. "Oh, I almost forgot..." He held up a small purple item in a Ziploc bag. I walked closer so I could see it better. "It wasn't wrapping paper, after all. Forensics found traces of chocolate, so they're suspecting it's a chocolate bar wrapper." He held out the Ziploc bag with the tiny swatch of wrapper we'd found down the bank by Mile Marker 18.

"What are you two talking about?" Amber asked. She followed us outside to see. Even Hunch made his way out my open front door to sniff out any new evidence. She looked back and forth between our faces and then at the swatch of wrapper in the Ziploc. "Wait, that looks like a Frucao wrapper."

Alex and I both looked at her. Hunch sniffed the air up toward the Ziploc, and Alex dropped it down near his thigh so my cat could get a better whiff.

"What's a Frucao?" I asked.

Amber shrugged. "It's a chocolate bar Lupe's mom sends her from Mexico every once in a while. She usually gets a bunch at a time, so Mom makes her give one to me and one to Danny."

I could definitely see how Lupe may have seen the Montrose kids as entitled. I glanced at Alex, but he was already onto another question. "And these were delivered to your house?"

Amber shrugged again. "All Lupe's mail comes to our house. I don't know why, really. But come to think of it, she hasn't given us a Frucao in ages. I bet Nando's hogging them all for himself."

"Nando likes the Frucao chocolate bars as well?" I asked.

"Yeah. It's different than the chocolate bars you find here in the grocery store. Frucao's got this spicy—" Amber stopped when she seemed to clue in that we couldn't possibly be this interested in comparisons between national chocolate brands. "Wait, where did you get that?" She motioned to the Ziploc bag.

I nodded. "Out by Mile Marker 18. On the bank near the hole."

Amber's eyes widened. "Lupe." She drew out the whispered name.

"It's just a candy bar wrapper, or a piece of one," Alex said. "Certainly nothing to rest this case upon, and as you said, Amber, both you and your brother also like Frucao bars. Maybe your dad did, too."

"No, Dad never ate chocolate. He didn't even like sweets."

But I understood. Amber needed someone other than her mom and brother to look at as possible suspects.

"We'll get over there and talk to Lupe first thing tomorrow morning," I told Alex. Then I turned to Amber. "Are you going to be able to hold it together to ask a few questions without throwing blame around?"

"Pfft. I did fine with my brother, and with Mom's charity workers, didn't I?"

"She did that," Alex said, backing away toward his driver's door again. "Amber's got this. Just ask a few probing questions and then we can put our heads together about it later."

Truthfully, I should probably be more concerned about my own ability to ask casual nonthreatening questions, as I seemed to keep messing that up, even with Amber.

Throughout the rest of the evening, as I taught Amber to mix and bake an easy zucchini muffin recipe, I practiced a few casual leading conversation starters in my head.

Do you have any chocolate, Amber? I have a real craving. Maybe Lupe knows where some is?

Oh, hey, Lupe, I heard you were here when Mrs. Montrose came home and had to tell Danny about his dad being flattened like a pancake. That must have been awful!

Then again, maybe I'd better let Amber take the lead on this.

She'd also been deep in thought through most of our cooking class and later, as I got her settled into the guest room, but first thing the next morning, she let me in on her mental process.

"So if Lupe borrowed the Tesla and, for some reason, drove it out to Mile Marker 18, left a chocolate bar wrapper down the bank in the mud, and then ran over my dad, first of all, why would she do that? My dad was the one who paid her salary. He's the one who hired her. Twice!" she added.

"Twice?" I asked.

"Yeah, she used to be my parents' housekeeper years ago. When Mom got pregnant with Danny, she'd been on bed rest for most of it, so he'd hired a fulltime nurse that took over as housekeeper. I guess Lupe went back to Mexico and got married, but when that didn't work out, she came back asking my dad for a job again."

"And how long ago was this?" I asked, trying to get a full picture.

Amber looked up at the kitchen ceiling. "About four years ago, I think. Dad fired our other housekeeper, Emily, because he'd always liked Lupe."

I nodded, thinking this over, but Amber went right back to her train of thought on the night of the accident.

"Also, why would my mom or brother have taken the car into Mel Stanley, because I'm pretty sure Lupe wouldn't have been able to bring the car in and put it under my parents' name?"

"You're certain about that?" I asked. I grabbed two zucchini muffins for each of us, and we headed for the Prius. On the way there, I checked my phone and had a new text from Alex.

~Cade's alibi checks out. The manager at stu's convenience store knew him by name and said he was hanging around talking to friends outside the store last monday. He figured he was there for an hour or more. Was driving a bright green car.~

I quickly clicked my phone off before Amber could catch sight of the text. It might be better to have her continue thinking of her brother's friend as a suspect until we could at least confirm her brother's alibi. "What if Lupe came into the shop claiming that your mom had sent her to get a car fixed?"

Amber twisted her lips. "I guess it's possible, but I still don't get why Lupe would have wanted to kill or even hurt Dad. He was the nicest to her of anybody."

I backed out of my driveway, again with Hunch on Amber's lap, and headed up the hill toward her neighborhood.

"Hmm, well, maybe she didn't mean for it to happen. Maybe somehow she didn't see him, hopped out of her car to see if he was okay, and that's when a piece of chocolate bar wrapper swept out onto the road's shoulder?"

"And all the way down near the hole?" Amber shook her head. "It still doesn't explain why someone dug the hole, though, does it? Or why FDS was carved into the tree."

She was right about that. Right about all of it. When I couldn't fall asleep last night, I'd lain in bed, doodling in my notepad and going over all of the various clues and oddities we'd discovered regarding Dan Montrose's death. I had spent a lot of time deliberating on what FDS could possibly stand for. The closest I had come was with Danny's first two names—Daniel Seth. But what was the F for? Some kind of expletive?

"Well, we have a lot of things to ask Lupe about then, don't we?" I said. "Let's just take it slowly and try not to raise her suspicions of why we're asking." I reached for Hunch, and he let out a low growl, but I adopted my sternest voice to tell him, "Mrs. Montrose is allergic to you, buddy. This is one stop where you won't be able to help investigate."

But Hunch hissed at me, not having any of it. He didn't like being stuck in the car, and who would? But then Amber, his new BFF, came to my cat's rescue. "Mom'll never know if Hunch stays in the backyard for a bit." She held him up so she could look at him eye to eye, a dangerous feat with a regularly hissing cat if you asked me. "Only if you promise not to wander off?"

Hunch gave her a sweet little mewl in reply, and I supposed that settled it. We headed down the street to the Montrose mansion with Hunch in Amber's arms.

Amber led the way around the side of their yard, the same route we had taken when we snuck out during the wake. Once we made it into their yard, she let Hunch down near the back porch, and he immediately started sniffing every plant and blade of grass in the vicinity. With a good quarter acre of flower gardens, flawless green grass, and lawn furniture to investigate, I was fairly confident we'd find Hunch still nosing around by the time we returned. Besides, as it had been when Cooper had been alive, Hunch wouldn't wander far with an investigation afoot.

I tiptoed behind Amber into the mudroom, and it was a good thing we were quiet because the door to the kitchen was open a couple of inches, and we immediately heard voices. Amber silently crept forward, and I followed in her footsteps.

At first, I didn't recognize the lady in jeans and a black blouse that Helen Montrose was speaking to through the gap of the open doorway. But then the lady turned, and familiarity struck. Her legs didn't look quite as good in jeans, and her black hair seemed flat without the bonnet, but this was unmistakably the Montrose housekeeper, Lupe, in plain clothes today.

I furrowed my brow, thinking Amber surely would have told me if it had been Lupe's day off. But only a moment later, Lupe spoke, stealing my attention.

"We stay through the will reading like you tell us. Now give me my money and we leave town. You never see us again."

Helen Montrose let out a humorless laugh, but nonetheless poised a checkbook onto the kitchen island and started to write. "You act like you haven't done anything wrong. I can't believe I'm paying you. *I* didn't kill Dan."

Lupe dug her fists into her waist. "No, his son kill him."

I froze in place, and because I was crouched so close to Amber in the doorway, I could actually feel her breath catch.

"Now, where me and Nando passports? He keep them in a safe some place here?" Lupe directed her eyes all around the kitchen. In an instant, Amber and I both glued ourselves to the mudroom wall, out of sight.

"Ha!" Helen said loudly in a tone that almost sounded like it contained some humor. "Dan never kept a safe, never trusted it, in case the police showed up with a search warrant one day. Dan buried things. If you'd known him at all, you'd have known that. Good luck finding your passports." She laughed again.

"Nobody did right in all this. Nobody." Lupe snatched the check out of Helen's hand and started to turn away.

In an instant, I grabbed Amber's arm and yanked her toward the back door and outside. Thankfully, a giant shrub right beside the back steps made the perfect hiding spot. Seconds later, the door opened and closed with a bang.

Through the shrub, I could make out Lupe's form. She wore red shiny high heels with her jeans and looked quite stylish for a housekeeper on her day off. Or now that I thought about it, it wasn't simply a day off, was it? This was her day of termination.

Her heels clacked along the cement path until a moment later when they stopped in place. I peered closer into the shrub to see what she had stopped for, and then my breath stilled. Hunch, just off the path in the flower bed, was kicking up dirt.

"Pierdase!" Lupe hissed at Hunch and kicked one of her red shoes at him.

Hunch moved quickly away from her shoe and then skittered off to hide behind a nearby azalea bush. When I turned back, Lupe had crouched onto her knees and was digging with her hands in the dirt where Hunch had been.

It didn't take long for her to find something. Less than a minute later, she stood, brushed off her hands and then her jeans, and picked up a dirty Ziploc bag—this one had two navy objects inside. They looked like passports.

The eyeline through the shrub wasn't great, but nonetheless, the grin that spread across Lupe's face couldn't be missed.

Chapter Sixteen

AS SOON AS LUPE had cleared the backyard, we gathered Hunch up, and Amber pulled me toward the neighbor's fence. "I think we should follow her," she said. "Come on, this is faster!"

Faster, true, but quite the obstacle course, with decorative rocks and shrubs to navigate around, and as we scaled a wooden fence, which Hunch and Amber both had a much easier time clearing than I did, it reminded me I wasn't fifteen anymore.

Even though I still wasn't certain of why we should follow Lupe, with so much to sort out from the last fifteen minutes, I was more than willing to let Amber call the shots for the moment.

By the time we reached my car, I figured we must have lost her, but Amber told me, "Don't worry, there's a long traffic light at the bottom of the hill. Takes forever to go green. We'll catch up."

And we did.

Once in clear view of Lupe's navy Ford Focus, Amber shook her head ruefully. "I should have had my voice recorder on."

But would she have wanted to have proof that it was actually her brother who killed her dad? Of course I didn't spell this out, but I probably should gently bring up Alex and how we eventually needed to be honest with him about everything.

"Wait, Lupe has a dark blue car?" I blurted, the thought suddenly coming to me. Even though Lupe had just stated the identity of the person who had struck down Dan Montrose, I couldn't help grasping for the rest of the truth. Had Danny taken his mom's Tesla that night? Or Lupe's car, to try and frame her for his dad's murder?

"Yeah, I don't know why I didn't think of it. Maybe because it's barely ever at our house. It used to be Danny's, but our dad hadn't wanted him to buy the Corvette and waste all his time trying to rebuild it. So when he went ahead and bought it anyway, Dad went ballistic and gave Danny's car to Lupe. Danny's had to beg to borrow my parents' cars or take the bus ever since."

Motive. Nothing but motive.

"Where do you think she's going?" I asked because the direction Lupe turned made my stomach tighten for a whole other reason.

"If it were me and I'd just gotten some kind of huge check from my mom, I'd hit the nearest bank," Amber said. She didn't notice how the word "bank" shook me as she ran her fingers all the way from Hunch's neck to his tail. He lapped up the affection, both of them oblivious to my distress. She went on about Lupe. "She's lying, you know. There's no way Danny did this. She's just trying to pin it on him, and my mom's too out of it to realize the truth."

It made more sense now why Amber didn't seem to be a mess over this new information. I didn't know if I agreed, but all I could think of was the word "bank," coupled with the direction we were heading. The bank Cooper had died in was just around the corner from here. As the bank came into view, my breath caught. Lupe pulled into the parking lot of the strip mall where it was located.

I hadn't been back here in almost eight months. In fact, besides surveying the site shortly after his death, I'd made a concerted effort not to drive down this particular street.

The last time I'd set eyes on the structure, the façade of brick had been blackened, with half of the roof collapsed. Now the bank and the shops on either side of it were barely recognizable, with brand new stucco walls and much more modern-looking signage.

I swallowed. It made my insides turn that I hadn't been back again before they made the changes. I hadn't gotten one more look at where Cooper had spent his last moments.

"See, she's going inside," Amber said, breaking me from my thoughts.

I still wasn't exactly sure why we were following her. "Do you think we should follow her inside?" I asked, even though I couldn't imagine many places I'd less like to go.

Amber shook her head. "Nah, but let's see where she goes after this. See where she lives, just so we know."

Again it seemed odd—and maybe a tad entitled—that Amber had no clue where the housekeeper who had been working in her home for years lived. But I nodded. I didn't have another plan, and at this point, I needed any thoughts that might distract me.

I had just started to sort through my thoughts about why Lupe, Helen, and Danny might have been in on covering up Dan Montrose's murder together when Amber said, "That's where her son, Nando, works." She pointed across the strip mall parking lot to a small Mexican restaurant called La Cortina.

"Right. *He'd* had Lupe's car the night of the accident because he had to work." I'd reverted to calling it an accident with Amber. It seemed gentler than saying *the night your dad died.* Or worse, *the night your dad was murdered.* "So they must live far enough away from here that he wouldn't have been able to walk."

I was still piecing it all together, but at least I'd figured out that Danny must have used his mom's Tesla the night of the accident.

"Maybe you should go and check to make sure he was on shift last Monday night," Amber suggested. "To make sure he definitely had Lupe's car." She was clearly still pulling at any possible threads that could exonerate her brother. "If he's working now, it would seem weird if I did it."

But fruitless or not, the idea of going anywhere so I didn't have to sit here staring at the new face of the bank spurred me on, and I eagerly grabbed for my purse. "Did Nando have anything against your dad?" I reached for the door handle.

Amber shrugged. "Don't think he liked any of us, but he was hardly ever at our house. You know, at least before my dad died."

This didn't surprise me. Besides, if Lupe considered the Montrose kids entitled, it made sense that Nando would feel that way, too.

Amber said, "I'll give the horn three quick honks if Lupe comes back, though, because if she's spouting lies about Danny, it's probably more important to follow her."

Amber's brain processed all of this much quicker than mine. I had been used to that with Cooper, and it brought back a strange sort of nostalgia.

As I walked across the parking lot, I thought back to when I'd sat across from Cooper many times in our college library. I'd help to research specific murder weapons or police procedures for one of his new novels. I'd only have to read a small paragraph out loud for Cooper, and seconds later, his hands would fly into a frenzy over his laptop as though his mind had pieced together a hundred new plot ideas from the one paragraph.

The door to La Cortina opened with a middle-aged couple leaving as I arrived. They held the door open, and I walked inside to see bright blue walls with orange leather booths. A number of velvet, gold-adorned sombreros hung on the walls, as well as an upright beaded decorative iguana. The place was nearly empty, not surprising considering the time, barely eleven in the morning. One man sat alone at a booth, reading a newspaper and sipping a coffee. Otherwise, I was the only customer.

As I headed for the counter, I prepared my story. A bronze-skinned boy met me on the other side. This boy was taller and had fuller cheeks than Nando. "Can I help you?"

I glanced down and his nametag read: MATEO. "Um, yeah." I looked at the backlit menu above him. "A week ago, on Friday the thirteenth, I came in and had a great platter that the guy who took my order recommended, but I can't remember which one it was. Were you working last Friday?"

The boy looked up, searching his memory. "Yeah, but I don't remember recommending anything." He stared at me, not offering to help beyond that.

"Was there anyone else who you know was working last Friday?" I asked. "It was in the evening."

The guy raised an eyebrow, seemingly in disbelief that I would push this issue and not just order. Finally, he turned and yelled through the food warmers into the back kitchen prep area. "Anyone know if they were working last Friday night?"

He didn't wait for an answer, but instead grabbed a clipboard from the wall, flipped through it toward the back, and as he did, glimpses of different pages indicated it was daily listings of who had been staffing the place. The oldest ones seemed to be at the back of the clipboard.

Thank goodness for places that weren't as technologically advanced as they could be.

When the boy returned to meet me at his till, he said, "Don't think so. I was the only one here. So, uh, did you want to order something?"

I ordered a platter #4, barely paying attention to what it contained. I kept glancing at that clipboard, which the boy had hung back on the wall. He gave me the total, and I had just enough cash to pay for it. As he gave me my small amount of change, I had an idea.

"Oh, but I'm allergic to paprika, so can you make sure they don't use any spice blends with paprika in them? And I'd also like some jalapenos, but on the side, and only cheddar for the cheese, if you wouldn't mind." When he didn't immediately move, I added, "But the paprika is the most important thing. No paprika anywhere near my dish, please. I'm anaphylactic."

I could sense the boy's eye roll, even if he didn't offer one outright. Thankfully, though, my annoying requests had the desired effect, and he headed back toward the kitchen to have a conversation with the cooks. I glanced quickly at the man with the newspaper, but his gaze stayed on the article he was reading.

I took two stealthy steps sideways and pulled the clipboard from the wall in one fluid motion. There wouldn't be much time, so I didn't look up again until I found last Friday's date. The pages were all looped around two giant rings at the top, and I decided in an instant that I wouldn't have time to either take the page off properly or snap a photo. Instead, I ripped it quickly from the two rings.

I was shoving the page into my purse with one hand while replacing the clipboard with the other when Mateo's voice sounded, coming back around the warming units. "All our spice mixes have paprika, so it might be kind of flavorless."

I let out my breath. Thankfully, he hadn't noticed me with the clipboard or my new position at the counter. "Oh, that's okay!" I let out a loud laugh to cover my nervous voice. "I'm used to flavorless food."

The boy headed back to the kitchen to tell the cooks to go ahead with my order, but that's when three quick honks sounded from across the parking lot.

It looked like I wouldn't be having flavorless tacos after all.

Chapter Seventeen

IT HADN'T BEEN A mistake to steal the La Cortina schedule. I double-checked the date, Friday, August 13th, but Nando Sanchez could not be found anywhere on the page for the date of Dan Montrose's death.

I made a quick right as Amber relayed this information. We had almost lost Lupe by the time I had raced across the parking lot and started up the Prius, but now I caught sight of her dark blue car with its signal on, two traffic lights ahead.

"You're sure he didn't have another job anywhere else?" I asked Amber.

"Pretty sure. Whenever Lupe talked to her mom on the phone, she always bragged about how Nando was working his way up to assistant manager at the Mexican restaurant." She let out a low chuckle and added, "I don't think Nando was nearly as proud of his mom and her job. I heard him more than once telling her she shouldn't be working as someone's maid—she was better than that." Amber shook her head. "Ridiculous. My dad paid her really well to take care of our house."

"Like, how well?" I asked. Lupe's jeans and shiny red heels had looked like designer brands. I turned another corner to follow Lupe, and she surprisingly started climbing back into the hills again—into a different wealthy neighborhood. This wasn't near the Montrose mansion, but these places were larger than my big house and seemed to have equally nice views.

Amber shrugged. "I dunno, but probably several thousand. And it's not like she had expenses. She ate at our house. She did her laundry and got her mail there." Amber looked ahead of us up at the large houses. "Although, I guess if she lives up here, that might be her problem." Amber crinkled her forehead like she didn't understand why Lupe and Nando would live up the hill in this ritzy neighborhood on a housekeeper's income.

"We don't know that she's going home," I said, weaving around a corner to keep Lupe in my sights, without getting too close. "Maybe she's visiting someone."

Amber smirked. "Ha. Maybe Lupe has some hot, rich man on the side."

If that were the case, I suspected this would be a goodbye visit. Lupe, after all, had just promised Helen Montrose she would soon be leaving town. "I should have asked if Nando gave his notice at La Cortina," I said.

Just then, Lupe made a sharp right into a driveway. I sailed by her in order not to draw her attention. Once around the next bend and out of sight, I stopped and took a breath. Thankfully, there was no one behind me. I looked around for somewhere to park, but in this part of the neighborhood, there weren't a lot of shoulder options. It seemed you'd have to know someone to park in one of these giant driveways.

I headed up the hill farther and eventually found a shoulder spot I could fit my Prius into. Once parked, I turned to Amber. "Now what?"

She shrugged. "Want to go back and sneak around a little?"

I didn't, really. I'd never had much ability to stay calm in these high-stress type of situations, but if Amber was willing and eager, I supposed I should be, too. I certainly wasn't about to let her snoop around alone.

Hunch, again, growled at the idea of holding down the fort in my car. He followed us, creeping low to the ground as we wound our way back down the hill toward the driveway we'd seen Lupe pull into. Her car wasn't in the main driveway, it turned out, but instead off to the side on a gravel patch. There were no other cars in the driveway.

"Maybe she cooks or cleans for someone else?" I suggested.

"Doubt it," Amber said. "She's usually at our house from eight in the morning until ten at night, six days a week."

I looked up at the large house in front of us. It had to be three stories, covered in stucco. Even though not as large as the Montrose mansion, it was far bigger than the house I found too big to live in alone.

Amber stepped forward, eager to investigate, but I held her back behind a nearby neighbor's motorhome for a minute. "I'm going to text Alex what we've found so far and where we're at. You know, just in case."

Amber anxiously tapped her fingers on the motorhome as it took me several minutes to update Alex on the conversation we'd overheard between Helen Montrose and her former housekeeper, Nando's alibi with his mom's car that hadn't checked out, and the address of where we had followed Lupe to.

When I slipped my phone away, Amber said, "So soon?" in her usual sarcastic tone.

I rolled my eyes at her, and we moved stealthily onto the next house. We ducked beside Lupe's blue Ford for a minute to take in the house a little better. It was even bigger close up, with wide stairs leading up to large double oak front doors. I peeked through the windows of Lupe's car while Amber surveyed the exterior.

"It's a nice car for a housekeeper," I whispered to Amber, but then remembered it had been Danny Jr.'s. It was probably a few years old, but now that I looked inside, it came with a navigation system and smartphone hookups. I hadn't opted for those options in my Prius because of the price hike. Apparently, Amber hadn't been kidding about her parents paying their housekeeper well, not to mention these kinds of perks. Which begged the question of why on earth this lady would want to literally kill the hand that had been feeding her.

I tiptoed around to the front of the car. Even though whichever vehicle had hit Dan Montrose had likely been into Mel Stanley's repair shop the very next day, I wondered if there might still be any evidence to the fact.

Amber crouched behind me and ran a thumb over where the fender met the headlight. "Does this paint look different to you than the paint on the hood?"

I squinted and studied it closer. It was certainly possible, but then again, it could have been the glare of the sun that made the fender paint look shinier. I peeked at the undercarriage and closer at the windshield. Even though I'd read about how to check if a car had been in an accident—more research for Cooper's novels—I didn't know enough about cars to actually decipher any of it myself.

Out of the corner of my eye, movement caught my attention, but it was only Hunch. He was creeping along the side of the big house as though he had found something, or at the very least, he was searching for something specific.

I tiptoed between Lupe's car and the side of the house, following my cat deeper toward the backyard. Hunch had, after all, led Lupe to the exact spot in the Montrose garden to find a buried baggie of passports.

"Where are we going?" Amber whispered from behind me.

I shrugged and pointed to Hunch, who barreled ahead in a way that only a cat without any fear of trespassing could.

The house appeared even bigger from the side than it had from the front. While the Montrose mansion had been on a large plot of land, complete with mature trees and sculpted shrubs, this house only had room for a small cement walkway along the side of the house before a neighbor's fence. There would be no hiding if someone appeared at either end of the walkway and caught us here.

Thankfully, we made it to the other end quickly. The backside of the house contained a small patch of grass, and my eyes quickly surveyed it, looking for my cat.

Amber tapped me on the shoulder and pointed, and that's when I saw him, halfway up a set of wooden back stairs. I looked back at Amber, and in silent agreement, we moved forward after Hunch.

We had almost made it to the top of the stairs when voices came through a screen door.

"I don't care how many millions you got out of that two-faced corrupt family," a young male voice said. "*This* is my home. Go to Mexico if you want. Now that I have my passport, I don't have to work for some stupid distant uncle anymore. I can get my own job. I'm staying right here."

I looked back at Amber with wide eyes. She mouthed the name, "Nando."

I let Amber squeeze closest to the door while I backed down one stair and silently pulled out my phone. I shot Alex a quick text:

~I think you should get over here ASAP!~

Lupe's voice came next. "Here? How you think you're going to stay here, *hijo*? You think Mr. Montrose is going to keep paying our rent from his grave? You know how much a place like these cost in the real world when somebody isn't taking care of you?"

Thanks to Amber's earlier suggestion, I fumbled over my phone to find my voice recording app. And just in time, too, as Nando really let loose all of his thoughts to his mom.

"Pfft! Taking care of us? You think that man cared at all about us, Mamá? It was hush money for your little secret that you kept with him. You acted like we'd come live in America and start our own life, our own business like Uncle Carlos—"

"I try—" Lupe started to say, but Nando wouldn't let her.

"But that was never what you planned on, was it, Mamá? I'm tired of keeping secrets, and I'm tired of living like we need some rich *bolillo* treating us like slaves. I never needed no fancy house. I never needed him to admit to being my papá. That was all you."

His...papa? I looked at Amber, but her attention remained rapt on the screen door.

"Fernando Daniel Sanchez!" Lupe dropped her voice, and it turned to begging. "*Please!*"

I couldn't make out the rest of her words through the screen door as she went on, and neither could Amber apparently because she slowly depressed the thumb pad on the door and inched it open. I held my breath, but I was pleased with how silently she managed it. I caught a few more of Lupe's hushed words now: "No tell anyone" and "policía" and "*Abuela* in Querétaro."

But Nando's name kept echoing in my head. Fernando Daniel Sanchez. Fernando Daniel Sanchez. And suddenly it hit me—FDS!

While I concentrated on hearing and deciphering, I didn't notice Hunch sneak by me, and then by Amber, through the open door, and into Lupe and Nando's kitchen, until I saw a last flick of his tail.

"Shoot!" Amber whispered back to me. She ducked onto her hands and knees, inched the door open wider, and crawled forward to retrieve my nosy, rule-breaking cat. She had made it all the way into the kitchen, with only one foot still in the gap of the screen door, when suddenly Nando's loud callous laugh made me freeze in place.

"Well, well. What do we have here? If it isn't sweet and innocent Amber Montrose. What? Is she breaking and entering into my home? That couldn't possibly be true, could it?" He let out another laugh, this one closer to maniacal. "Should I call the police to come and get her?"

My first instinct was to launch forward toward the screen door and somehow get in between Amber and what sounded like a mentally unstable brother she hadn't known she had, but as I took a step forward, Amber pulled her foot from out of the screen door, and it slammed shut.

The loud sound stopped me in place, and I took a breath, quickly rethinking my plan. If Nando truly was off his rocker, and if he had killed Dan Montrose in cold blood, maybe I should go for help.

As if to prove my point, Nando said, "I have a better idea. I killed one Montrose. No skin off my back to kill another. And don't worry, I'll make it look like an accident—or no, better yet, a suicide!" His voice sounded self-congratulatory. "Poor little rich girl couldn't handle her daddy's death..."

"Fernando, no!" Lupe hissed from farther away. I still couldn't hear her voice well, and I suspected she was keeping her distance from both Amber and her crazy son. "You can't do this! Not again! I cannot fix this time!"

"Shut up and get me the zip ties from the toolkit," he snapped at his mom.

I tiptoed down one stair and then another, hoping my voice recorder was still doing its job. But when I stepped onto the third stair, it let out a creak, and I froze in place.

"What? Who's there?" Nando asked sharply. "Did you bring someone with you?"

Two thudding steps sounded in the kitchen above me toward the door. I held my breath and raced down another six steps two by two, knowing I wouldn't make it around the corner before he got outside and caught me.

But then a loud "Mrrreeooowww!" overtook all of my noisy steps, and as I raced to the bottom and around the corner, all I heard was Nando yelling, "Owwww! Get this thing off me!"

I waited around the corner, thankful for Hunch's distraction. I hoped his diversion had given Amber a chance to get away. But Hunch let out a loud yelp and then, seconds later, a loud whining sound from much closer.

Ten seconds passed. Then twenty. Only the ongoing whining of my poor cat. No Amber.

I moved farther down the side of the house until I was out of hearing range. I stopped my voice recorder, forwarded the recording to Alex, and then hit dial on his contact.

He had barely said hello when my words barreled over one another to get out of my mouth. "It's him! Nando Sanchez killed Dan Montrose, and now he's got Amber! He wants to kill her, too!"

"Wait, what? Okay, Mallory, breathe. Tell me where you are. Are you at the same address you texted me?"

I nodded, even though he couldn't see it, and eventually got a "Yes" through my dry, parched mouth.

"And he has Amber in the house? And he threatened to kill her?"

I nodded again. "Their suite is hidden away, up a back stairway of this house. I think he zip-tied her arms and maybe her legs. I sent you the voice recording, but I have to get back in there. What if he's doing it now?"

"No, Mallory, no. If that's his home and he has her tied up, he's probably not in a hurry to do anything right there, especially if others live in another part of the house. You need to stay out of sight. Find a place to hide. I'm on my way."

Chapter Eighteen

THE NEXT FIVE MINUTES were the longest of my life. I found a shed in the backyard to hide behind, and from there, I caught flashes of Nando and Lupe arguing through an upper kitchen window, but I had no idea if they had Amber tied up on their kitchen floor—or if she was even still okay.

And Hunch was most definitely not okay. After his diversion, Nando had seemingly kicked my cat out the screen door and down the twelve stairs onto the grass. He'd been yowling in pain ever since, and his left leg lay at an odd angle. Cats were known for landing on their feet, and if any cat had more cat skills than all the rest, it was Hunch. For him to have been injured in a fall, I had to guess that Nando had kicked him really hard.

I wanted so badly to go and check on him, to pull him back behind the shed with me to safety, but I knew better.

The sound of the screen door whipping open took my attention from my yowling, pained cat. Nando stood in a wide-set power stance in the doorway, feet braced apart with hands on his hips, surveying the cat and then the otherwise quiet yard. I stayed perfectly still, and he didn't look my way. "I'll take care of this, Mamá. You just call *Abuela* and tell her our home is here and we have every right to stay. I'm making sure of it."

He yanked Amber through the screen door and down the stairs. She had duct tape over her mouth and her hands were bound behind her back with zip ties, but relief washed over me to see her still living and breathing.

But that thought vanished quickly when he shoved her around the side of the house toward Lupe's car.

I had no idea where he was taking her!

I raced out from behind the shed, along the side of the house, and made it to the front yard what felt like an instant later, but only caught the exhaust of Lupe's car as Nando had already backed out and rounded the closest corner. Still no sirens, no sign of Alex. Then again, the police station was all the way on the other side of Honeysuckle Grove.

I splayed my hands out, at a loss of what to do. Only a second later, it came to me: Lupe!

I raced around the house and up the back stairs and found Lupe still in her kitchen, a small room considering the size of the house, weeping and speaking Spanish into her phone. My tenth-grade understanding of the language was no match for the speed that her words tripped out of her mouth.

"Hang up!" I told her. "Now!"

She was hunched over the kitchen counter and looked up at me in stunned silence. I took two giant steps toward her, grabbed her phone, and hung it up myself.

"You can't do anything about what your son did to Dan Montrose, but you can stop what he's about to do to his daughter." I didn't give her time to argue or even think about it. I hoped her mothering heart would be enough to lead her to do the right thing here. I yanked her toward the door and down the stairs, and thankfully, she didn't fight me.

At the bottom of the back stairs, I bent to check on Hunch. I gently prodded his back, and his yowling became louder as I touched his stomach. When I got to his hind leg, he made a low guttural growling sound. I lifted him from the ground, trying to keep that hind leg as still as possible, and cradled him in my arms.

"Don't worry," I said over his noises. "I'm going to take care of you, buddy. We just have to take care of Amber first."

As I pulled Lupe up the hill toward my car with my other arm, I asked her, "Where was Nando taking her? What were his plans?"

A fresh round of tears flooded her face. "I don't know! He don't say!"

My hope started to dwindle, but I tried to intercept its plunge. "We'll figure it out. Call him."

I motioned to her cell phone, and she hit a number to dial, but it rang and rang endlessly as we made our way to my car. While she focused on getting through to Nando, I pressed the call button on my phone in my pocket. The last person I'd dialed was Alex, so I hoped it would get through to him so he could overhear that we were on the move, without Lupe knowing.

As we got into my Prius, she finally hung up her phone, and I said, "As I drive, you tell me every single thing Nando said to you."

I propped my phone upside down in my cupholder. If Alex had said anything on the other end, it must have been while the phone was in my pocket. Thankfully, he stayed silent now. As I drove us down the hill where I'd seen Lupe's car disappear, Lupe rattled off frantic clips of sentences, whatever she could remember from her son. I kept reminding her that she was saving her son's well-being as much as she was saving Amber.

As she talked, I pieced together the details of Nando's anger. Nando had only just found out that Dan Montrose was his father last Friday. He'd threatened to go public, to which Dan threatened to reveal a police file he had on Lupe.

"What police file?" I asked.

"I think he getting work visas for us, but he only steal our passports and then plant drugs on me to get caught. I not use drugs ever, but Dan make it look like I do and call the police, then once I arrested, he pay off police to let me out. He say he have to bribe them not to put me in jail. But he keep file on me. He say if I keep my mouth shut that he Fernando's father, he find us place to stay and give me police file and passports back when Nando turn eighteen so we go back to Mexico."

Mile Marker 18. That was the significance.

Lupe went on to describe the night Dan had died. He usually never came home before dark, so Nando had been watching a movie in the Montrose's theatre room. When Dan returned earlier than expected, he was already in some kind of a bad mood. Then he lit into Lupe about keeping "her Mexican kid" out of his house and she'd better not have told anyone he was Nando's father. Apparently, Nando heard it all.

Then when Nando threatened to go public about Dan being his father, Dan rushed off to dig up the police file, saying he was going to have her and her Mexican kid deported once and for all.

"Nando follow him, and after he dig up the file, Nando drive into him." Lupe let out a fresh round of tears into her hands. "He come back, and at first, he tell me he hit a deer, so I fix the car."

It wasn't until Nando, who could read English a lot better than Lupe, looked at the so-called police file after he'd killed Dan that they realized it had all been a ruse to scare Lupe. The file was just a bunch of papers with her name on them. The police officers who'd pulled her over had been in plain clothes and in a dark unmarked car, likely not real cops.

Once I had that part figured out, I grilled her about the earlier details. "I don't get it. How did you have a baby so close in age to Danny Jr. without anyone knowing?"

She shook her head and looked into her lap. "Years ago, I think I love Dan Montrose. He act like he love me, too, but then I get pregnant and I about to tell him when he say Helen is pregnant with a precious son but she have to be on bed rest. He hire a new nurse and fire me that same day. I return to Mexico and try to raise Nando with another man, but he beat us, so finally I come back to tell Dan about his son. He never want to accept it."

I shook my head, taking all of this in. Amber knew her dad hadn't been an upstanding guy, but I had a feeling she would be pretty shocked at the extent of his secrets and lies.

Providing I found her in time to tell her.

"He always threaten me if I ever mention what really happen, he have me arrested and deported for good. I could never come back to see my brother, Carlos, again."

I shook my head, wondering what all that information would have done to a seventeen-year-old boy. But even though Nando had killed Dan Montrose in a fit of rage after he found out what must have been some pretty shocking news, Lupe could still prevent him from becoming a serial killer without a conscience. Or his anger could completely consume him.

"Where would he take Amber Montrose?" I asked in as calm of a voice as I could manage.

"He say he would take care of her. Is all he say!" Lupe cried.

"Think! Where could he have taken her in the middle of the day where no one would see or hear what he was doing?" I glanced at my phone in the cupholder. "Would he have taken Amber out to the same place? To Mile Marker 18?"

She shook her head. "I no think so. Fernando is a smart boy. He say he make it look like an accident."

Suicide was the word I remembered, but I needed to keep her talking.

"Where did he hang out when he wasn't at home or working? Where might he go to be alone?"

She shook her head, but then stopped mid-shake. "We used to go to bridge off old closed-down highway. He used to say it was our spot because no one else knew about it."

"Old highway? Where? Not the Old Mission Highway?" I didn't know Honeysuckle Grove well enough to know these details. Lupe directed me, and I could only hope she was being truthful with me and not leading me off the trail so Nando could get away with killing Amber.

As I turned the Prius away from town and the roads became more and more deserted, I also became concerned for my own safety. The truth was, if Lupe and Nando got rid of both me and Amber, neither of them would have to be responsible for anything they had done.

Of course they didn't know about Alex listening in.

Hunch let out a low yowl that made me wonder if he had the same concerns. I glanced over the seat and said, "It's going to be okay, Hunch. We're going to find her."

Lupe instructed me to turn again at a faded wooden sign that read: HISTORIC HIGHWAY – OPEN TO FOOT TRAFFIC ONLY.

I ignored the instruction and forged ahead in my Prius on a bumpy road in great need of repair. "How far is the bridge?"

"Not far," she told me. Her brow furrowed, and she moved her head from side to side as though trying to see around corners before we turned them. "We usually walk. Is just around the next turn, I think."

In a split second, I pulled over to the edge of the unused road, hit the brakes, and stopped the car. We weren't going to surprise Nando if we pulled right up to the bridge in a vehicle.

But only a second later, Lupe launched out of the passenger door and ran ahead. I jumped out on my own side and ran after her, catching up and yanking her back by one arm just as she reached her own car, parked around the next bend at an angle in the middle of the road.

When I'd dragged her out of her kitchen, she had opted for some slip-on shoes, rather than the red heels, but I wore sneakers so it was unlikely she'd be able to outrun me even if she got away again. Besides, the farther we moved along the road, the more potholed it became.

Just as I had started to let out a breath of relief that we'd found their car and I'd caught Lupe, she opened her mouth and started yelling. "Fernando! Is us! She make me bring—"

I yanked Lupe's arm to shut her up, but it was too late. We'd no longer be able to sneak up on Nando. As Lupe's echoing words faded, it became eerily silent. He had said he'd make it look like a suicide. Had he already done it? Had he planned to throw Amber off the bridge?

I patted my pockets for my phone, but realized I'd left it in the cupholder of my car when I raced out after Lupe. It was up to me to do something to save Amber, and fast.

But as we moved in front of Lupe's car and farther around the corner, Amber was nowhere in sight on the pot-holed road or on the large wooden bridge in front of us. The flow of the current was thick and fast and headed back into town. Rocks protruded here and there, creating white water. This explained how Nando planned to make it look like a suicide if he threw her in here. She'd get tossed in every direction until someone spotted her ravaged, rock-beaten body closer to town.

Or didn't.

Although her bound arms would have to tip someone off that she hadn't done it herself.

I kept moving forward, onto the bridge, checking the rafters below, eying the expansive river underneath for a bobbing head, but there was nothing.

I gulped down a cry and kept moving forward, onto the slats of the bridge to get a closer look. I was so busy frantically scanning the water looking for Amber, it didn't occur to me that I hadn't seen Nando until he grabbed me around my neck from behind.

I shrieked, but he gripped me tighter to silence me. "I don't know who you are or what you want with me, but you are in the wrong place at the wrong time, senorita."

"No, Fernando, no!" Lupe said, crying, but she also wasn't fighting Nando in any way. She was going to let him do whatever he wanted to us.

I turned to her and pleaded, "You have to stop him, Lupe! Our blood is on your hands, too!"

"Shut up!" Nando snapped, but instead of pushing me farther onto the bridge, he yanked me away from it.

I fought him, swinging my arms and kicking my feet, but within seconds, he had me pushed up against a tree face-first, practically kissing the bark. I stopped fighting for a second and reached up to protect my face, but that seemed to be his plan because a moment later, he had both of my hands wrenched behind my back. Before I could blink, he had my hands secured tightly and painfully.

"Ow!" I winced. "You don't want to do this, Nando!"

Lupe was a crying mess and clearly not going to be of any help.

Nando, on a mission, didn't stop. He grabbed both of my legs and pinned both my ankles together to secure them with a zip tie, too. No matter how I struggled, he was stronger than me.

Thankfully, he hadn't seemed to bring any duct tape along, and so I kept talking. My voice might be my only weapon, and I intended to use it. "You may think you'll be able to live with this, but you won't. This will haunt you for the rest of your life." I turned to Lupe. "It'll haunt you both."

"Don't listen to her," Nando gritted out to his mother, "and stop your crying. These two aren't worth it."

Lupe, sadly, did as she was told, and her cries, or at least the volume of them, subsided. But then I heard a muffled sound, like a girl with her mouth covered, trying to call out.

"Amber?" My hope soared as the muffled sound became louder. The leaves shifted nearby. He hadn't thrown Amber into the water!

Nando motioned his chin into the trees and told his mother, "Go get her. These two obviously like to be together, so let's have them take one last swim together." Nando laughed—actually laughed—as though this were funny.

Lupe disappeared into the trees, leaving me with Nando. I watched his eyes as he checked over my ties and added a second zip tie to my wrists for good measure. Again, I wondered what it would do to a seventeen-year-old kid to realize your mom had been lying to you your entire life because your dad felt as if she was good enough to sleep with and clean his house, but not good enough to admit he'd impregnated her.

"What Dan Montrose did to your mom was wrong. Unforgiveable," I told Nando, trying a new tack. "There's no mistaking that he should have been arrested."

Nando laughed again. "Who cares? People like that don't get punished. Not unless people like me punish them." He shrugged as though this was everyday business. "I took care of it. Now I'm taking care of his nosy daughter, too. And I'll make sure she dies knowing what kind of person her daddy really was. Sorry you stuck your nose in and got in the way."

He didn't sound sorry in the least.

Lupe pulled Amber along behind her through the trees, still crying. Amber's mouth was still taped, so I suspected she hadn't been able to talk any sense into Lupe, and her wrists had scratches and streaks of blood from fighting against the zip ties.

"You've known Amber for years," I said, pleading with Lupe now. "Can you really let Nando—"

Nando yanked me away from the tree and pushed me toward the bridge, effectively shutting me up. I had to hop since my ankles were bound, and Lupe pulled Amber along behind us, without even being told to. She clearly felt she couldn't do anything to stop her out-of-control son.

I may not have had arms or legs, but I still had my voice, and I planned to use it until I no longer could. "You already killed the man who wronged you! Amber did nothing wrong. Let's make her understand why you had to do what you did, and then—"

"I said, shut up!" Nando pushed me so hard, I fell onto my knees on the bridge. They stung and then immediately ached in pain.

As he yanked me to my feet again, I said, "I'm not going to shut up because what you're doing is wrong and you know it."

He pushed me forward. "Talk all you want. No one can hear you out here!" He yelled the words as if to prove his point. "You're still going into the water, and so is Amber." He looked back to where Lupe pulled Amber along, but with much less force. Nando and I were almost in the middle of the bridge already, while Lupe and Amber had barely gotten a foot onto it. "Come on. Hurry it up, Mamá."

I shook my head at their strange mother-son relationship and had to wonder if it had been off-balance even before he found out about the lies. Nando pushed me up against the waist-high railing of the old rickety bridge. The one rotting wooden rail was all that kept me from falling into the tumbling river twenty feet below.

Could I at least somehow pull him in with me so he couldn't do this to anyone else?

But even if I could, his arms and legs weren't bound. There was a chance he'd be able to fight the current and swim to shore.

Nando turned back to his mother and had just growled in frustration when suddenly his growl stopped and his eyes widened. I followed his gaze to see Alex and his detective friend, both in uniform, sneaking silently from the nearest bush toward the bridge.

"Hold it right there!" Alex called. "Fernando Sanchez, get your hands in the air!"

He was about to comply with the order, or at least we all thought he was. But before Nando decided to oblige and get his hands into the air, he used them to give me one strong shove that knocked me up over the railing and headfirst into the water below.

Chapter Nineteen

So THIS WAS HOW I was going to die.

I tried to take in a huge breath and hold it, but it got knocked out of me the second I hit the water. As the ice-cold water enveloped me and the current pulled me under, I thought about the fact that Amber was safe, barely onto the edge of the bridge. I had at least managed that much. It might not get me into heaven, but it had to give me some credit with a God I rarely spoke to. I wondered absently if Hunch would make it through this day, too, or if we would both soon be reunited with Cooper in some kind of an afterlife.

The current tossed me around and continued to pull me under. My leg struck a sharp rock and stung, but only a second later, I couldn't feel it for the pressure engulfing my chest. Opening my mouth to the currents pulling me under would mean the end of me, but my chest and body ached with the effort of keeping it closed. My body's automatic response of trying to take a breath, even when there wasn't one to be had, seemed to take over.

I thrashed my bound arms and legs, trying to swim like a mermaid to get to the surface, but I no longer knew which direction was up. I opened my eyes, but they didn't help me one bit. The sparkly lights that had been behind my eyes a second ago morphed into something more like flashbulbs going off in my head, each one like a knife through my skull.

All I wanted, all I needed, was for this to end somehow. Blackness instead of lightbulbs, weightlessness instead of all this pressure.

I let my body take over. I had to, gasping for the breath that wasn't there.

And, finally, the blackness was exactly what I got.

My afterlife, as it turned out, didn't involve Cooper or Hunch. It only involved a lot of dark numbness. An endless amount of stillness.

It seemed like such a shame that I'd just started living again only to die. *God, why?* I asked inwardly. In that one prayer, I was asking Him about several things: How could He let Nando get away with this? Why had He taken Cooper from me so soon, when Cooper had been my only real link to spirituality? Why was He taking my life right at the moment when I finally had friends?

But then the stillness was interrupted some poking and prodding. Muffled voices. My weightless body felt as though it was rocking, back and forth, back and forth, back and...

All at once, fire ignited in my throat as a tsunami launched out of it.

"That's it," a deep male voice said. "Get it out."

I didn't want to get any more out, but my body was clearly listening to this man's instructions and not my own because a second later, another tidal wave of bile and water erupted from within me.

"Come on, open your eyes, Mallory!" the male voice said.

The thought wouldn't have occurred to me, but I tried it, and then regretted it immediately. The bright flashbulbs were back. But then something masochistic within me made me open my eyes again anyway, for as long as I could stand it, and slowly, the brightness became more manageable.

"It's all going to be okay now," the male voice that belonged to Officer Alex Martinez said from above me. He wiped my sopping wet hair from my face, and that's when I noticed he was just as wet. His hair was curlier than usual from the water, and even though I knew I shouldn't focus on that part, I couldn't seem to help myself.

Had Alex jumped into the river to save me?

"I guess swim club was a good idea after all," he said, as if in answer to my silent question.

Even though I suspected Alex's ability to save my life had more to do with rigorous police training than with seventh-grade swim club, the faint memory of sneaking into the bleachers at the local pool to watch twelve-year-old Alex swim laps brought with it the best kind of nostalgia.

Alex was in great shape. Swim club or no swim club, I had no doubt he would be capable of battling a raging river. I guess I just felt humbled and surprised that he'd do it for me.

"Amber?" I croaked out. "Is she okay?"

Alex smiled. "She's going to be just fine. Detective Reinhart is taking her down to the station to ask her a few questions. Lupe and Fernando are both in custody."

I started to let out my breath, but then it caught in my aching throat. "Hunch?"

Alex squinted down at me, but then surveyed the riverbank around us as though he fully expected to find my cat roaming somewhere nearby.

"In the backseat of my car," I told him. "He's hurt."

Alex nodded and stood. "I'll take care of it."

Before I could ask him anything else, or even thank him for saving my life, two paramedics appeared on either side of me. They checked my eyes, ears, and throat, which all felt like they'd recently been tossed into somebody's bonfire.

"We should take her in," one of them said.

"I'm fine," I argued, attempting to sit up. But I clearly wasn't, as the movement made my vision wobble and my head boom. I lay back down and let them move me to a stretcher.

It's all going to be okay now. I repeated Alex's words in my head, but I felt like it was going to take a long time before I'd believe them.

Chapter Twenty

THEY KEPT ME OVERNIGHT in the hospital, which didn't seem so bad, really. I kind of enjoyed having nurses come in and out of my room to check on me, all of them so kind and friendly, and even now I dreaded going back to my lonely house.

When Alex arrived later the next morning, I practically leaped for joy at his familiar face. He had changed into dry jeans and a blue button-down since yesterday, but even without the uniform, I could tell in an instant that this was all business.

"How's Hunch?" I asked, partly to soften the mood, but also because I was truly concerned.

Alex nodded. "His hip joint had to be reset and he's being fit for a cast on his back leg, but his stomach didn't suffer any permanent damage. He'll heal just fine."

"He's going to love dragging a cast around," I said sarcastically. Hunch had never had much patience for anything or anyone that slowed him down or got in his way.

"Regardless, you can pick him up at the vet as soon as you're released. The police department is picking up the bill."

Alex handed me a business card with the vet's information and cleared his throat. "I have a few questions to round out Reinhart's report."

"Reinhart's report? Isn't it your report?" I raised my eyebrows, but Alex looked down at the floor as he took a seat on the only chair in my small hospital room.

"Corbett says because I already signed off on this case, I can't put my name to any of this."

"Or get the credit," I added, already piecing together why Alex seemed so down when he should have been elated at proving himself as a competent detective. He didn't confirm or deny this, and because I didn't want to rub salt in the wound, I decided not to push the issue.

"So far, Fernando Sanchez hasn't been talking much. We've been able to make some sense of the situation from overhearing your conversation with his mother, Lupe, but we'd love your perception concerning the night Dan Montrose died."

I had been thinking of this nonstop since I was brought into the hospital. It gave me something to concentrate on while being poked and prodded. I thought I had most of it figured out.

"Nando overheard an argument with his mom and found out Dan Montrose was his father. Apparently, there was a contract, plus a police file on Lupe, keeping her quiet until Nando turned eighteen, and in exchange, he paid Lupe well and took care of all of their expenses. When Nando found out about everything and threatened to go public, Dan went out to dig up the police file at Mile Marker 18. I suspected he buried it there as a marker of Nando's eighteenth birthday—as Dan liked to commemorate dates along that highway. But Nando couldn't wait that long and followed him out there. He didn't even have to get his hands dirty to get the file—or at least he didn't at first. He stayed in his car until Dan climbed back up the hill and then ran into him and snatched the file out of his dead hands. When Lupe overheard Amber telling her brother about finding a hole out at Mile Marker 18, she called Nando, and he got right back out there to cover up the suspicious hole."

Alex nodded, writing it all down. "And do you figure he repaired the damage to his mom's car himself?"

I shook my head. "You may need a warrant, but if you check with a mechanic named Mel Stanley, I think you'll find that he completed the repairs. It looked like there could have been some mismatch in the paint on the front fender of Lupe's car. You could also check the code on the windshield, as well as the radiator and cooling lines to see if there had been any recent repairs to them."

Alex raised his eyebrows at me. "You know a lot about cars."

I felt a blush rise up my neck, but I had to admit the truth. "Actually, no. Nothing. I wouldn't know how to actually find any of those things myself, but I used to help with research on my husband's novels."

Alex shifted uncomfortably in his seat at the mention of my late husband. "Ah. Yes, well. I'm thankful for the insight, regardless."

In an instant, it felt like we had lost any comfortable camaraderie that had ever been between us. It reminded me that we had only known each other as adults for about three days. The saying *easy come, easy go* came to mind. Would Alex and I even continue our friendship now that I didn't need his help on an investigation? Not only that, but as he confirmed everything I had gone through at Lupe's house and then at the old highway bridge, our conversation became more and more a matter of business. It felt as though our whole reason for talking was quickly coming to an end.

In fact, my whole reason for being around other people quickly seemed to be coming to an end.

It wasn't as though I had enjoyed helping a fifteen-year-old through her grief, all while trying to solve the murder of her father, but something about it being over and done left me feeling lonely and purposeless already.

"All right, well, I think that's all I need." Alex flipped his book shut and stood, confirming my thoughts.

"You know where I am if there's anything else." I forced a smile up at him.

He headed for my hospital room door, but then stopped in the threshold of it. "You really were a huge help to me, Mallory. I can't thank you enough."

I nodded but couldn't bring myself to say anything for fear of crying. By tomorrow, I'd be back in my house, alone, with no reason to reach out to anyone.

But then he added, "If I ever come across anything else suspicious in Honeysuckle Grove, I know who I'd want to bring in as a special consultant." He winked, and just before he let the door fall shut behind him, he said, "You'll let me know when Hunch is feeling better and ready to work, huh?"

Chapter Twenty-One

A WEEK LATER, AS expected, I was back on my couch, covered in blankets, Netflix on my screen, and feeling about as lonely as I had in my whole life. Not only was Hunch annoyed with his cast, but he was also clearly annoyed with me. He pretty much spent his days across the room glaring in my direction.

I was tempted to call Amber and invite her over just to make my cat happy, but after all she'd been through with her family, all she had learned about them, I didn't want to be a reminder of that horrible time. I hoped she would somehow get past all of it and move on.

As I reached for the remote control from the coffee table, my phone lit up beside it with a new text. Odd. My sister and dad almost always phoned and rarely texted. I picked it up to look closer, and for a second, I was sure I must have somehow wished Amber back into existence in my life.

~So what about this cooking thing?~

I nibbled my lip, and tears of thankfulness filled my eyes. I hedged my hope, though, as I texted back.

~Your mom ok with that?~

A second later, an eye roll emoticon appeared on my screen. I wasn't sure I felt completely justified in corralling a fifteen-year-old for my own selfish reasons without her mom's knowledge or permission. Then again, her mom had just been an accessory in covering up her dad's murder to protect her inheritance. Maybe Amber needed a different adult figure in her life for a while.

But my fingers flew over the keys of my phone as if still determined to keep my hope at bay.

~I don't have much to work with at the moment.~

Thankfully, determination was a word Amber was familiar with.

~Meet you at the farmer's market in 20~

I smiled. It wasn't a question.

My smile flattened, though, as I looked down at myself. I hadn't showered in three days, and twenty minutes was most definitely not long enough to make me look presentable. However, I also didn't trust my texting fingers to ask for more time without pushing Amber away again. I hit two letters: OK. And then I raced up the stairs, likely making Hunch think I had lost my mind.

Twenty-two minutes later, I found Amber at the farmer's market's cheese counter looking over the array of options with a creased forehead. My wet hair stuck to my head, and my jeans hung loosely from forgetting to eat for the week, but at least I had checked for any errant pantyhose or other wardrobe malfunction before leaving the house.

"How do you choose from so many types?" Amber said in way of a hello. It reminded me of how good teenagers could be at skirting around any too-heavy emotional topics. I didn't know how badly I needed someone with that skill until right that second.

I pointed. "Well, start with the ones you know. What's the difference between cheddar and mozzarella, for instance?"

Amber shrugged. "Mozzarella's kind of flavorless."

Ahh, the girl had so much to learn about cheese. And I was exactly the person to teach her.

"Excuse me," I said to the clerk behind the cheese counter. And then I proceeded to order small amounts of a dozen different cheeses.

"What are we making?" Amber asked as we walked away with our cheese purchase.

I waved a finger in front of Amber's face. "Ahh, young Skywalker. Not *make*. Learn, you must."

Amber raised an eyebrow at my dorkiness, but she smiled just the same.

"We need a handful of other ingredients to make the cheeses pop," I told her, leading her toward a vegetable stand.

She stayed quiet as I picked out some bell peppers, a couple of habaneros, a yellow zucchini squash, and an eggplant. Even as we moved along to the fish market, the bakery counter, and then to pick up a few pieces of fruit, she remained silent.

It wasn't until we headed back to the Jeep, arms loaded with fresh groceries, that she finally opened her mouth again to speak. "Terrence Lane made partner at the firm. I guess the other partners didn't feel the same way my dad did about him. He's representing Mom and keeping us updated on what to expect. He figures it'll be several months before anyone goes to trial, but he says Lupe will definitely do jail time."

I couldn't read the mix of emotions leaking out in her voice. Satisfaction? Sadness? Relief?

"Just Lupe?" I asked. Had she somehow tried to take the blame for her off-kilter son?

"Thankfully, we get to keep the house since it was in Mom's name. We don't have boatloads of money or a housekeeper anymore, though, which is kind of annoying because Danny never learned to clean up a single thing after himself."

"Oh yeah?" I said. I wasn't sure if I should ask more about her mom, but hoped she felt free to keep talking.

"Terrence says the longer Nando's case takes to get to trial, the better it will work out. If he turns eighteen, they'll try him as an adult. Still, he'll probably try and plead down to voluntary manslaughter and get off with only a few years." Any fifteen-year-old who hadn't grown up with a lawyer for a father likely wouldn't have such a strong grasp on all of this. She blew out some air as I started to drive toward my house. She shrugged as though she'd already come to terms with the injustice of it and went on. "I mean, I know my dad wasn't a good guy, and maybe he deserved some kind of payback, but he didn't deserve to die." She sighed, and I was glad she could get some of this out. I suspected it was the first time she had. "I suppose I should be happy Nando was caught and will be punished at all."

"Well, that's thanks to you," I told her. "You'd make a pretty good detective one day."

She raised an eyebrow. "You think so?"

"I know so." I wouldn't actually wish for her to work under Captain Corbett's leadership, especially because he'd somehow made the lack of investigation of the Montrose case the fault of the detective originally assigned to it. After seeing Captain Corbett's lack of initiative with the case firsthand, I didn't believe it for one minute. I still didn't trust something about the man. For as long as I lived in Honeysuckle Grove, I'd be keeping an eye out for the police captain.

As Amber and I loaded the groceries into my kitchen, Hunch surprisingly didn't immediately come to greet us. Then again, it took him a lot more time and effort to move around with his cast.

"Why don't you go find Hunch," I told Amber. "Believe me, he'll be glad to see you."

I felt slightly embarrassed about my messy house. I hadn't bothered to pick up much after myself in the last week and had been too rushed to do anything on my way out the door, but I was so glad to have Amber here that I could push some of the embarrassment aside. And she didn't seem to notice or care.

Less than a minute later, she returned with Hunch awkwardly in her arms with his cast sticking out, but he purred in her arms. I went over and scrunched the fur on Hunch's head, hoping he would realize in his oversized cat brain that I was the one who went out and brought his best friend back.

Then again, Hunch was so intuitive, he likely knew that all the credit actually went to Amber.

As I laid out the cheeses and corresponding food items to help their flavors come alive, Amber sat at the kitchen table in her usual chair and kept Hunch happy. She opened the cookie container, but today it was empty. Later Amber could help me remedy that.

"Hey, are you going to the church picnic on Sunday?" she asked as I brought over the first pairing—a red pepper with warmed mozzarella.

After my debacle with the pantyhose and then that out-of-body volunteering episode, I hadn't been planning on going back to church for quite some time. "I hadn't thought about it. Why?"

She shrugged. "I kinda wanted to go, but I doubt my mom will want to." She took a bite, and her eyes widened at the taste.

"That's mozzarella," I told her. She squinted as though she didn't believe me. I was buying time as I thought over her request. If Amber wasn't bitter toward God and church after all she'd been through, why was I? Especially since I had so many questions for Him that still needed answers. "So...your mom? She's not going? To the picnic?" As usual, my prying questions came out as anything but casual and non-invasive.

But Amber, the intuitive girl I'd gotten to know pretty well in a short amount of time, answered what I was really asking. "She's spending her time doing community service because Terrence told her to, but to be honest, I think she loves it. It keeps her busy, and now that she's not getting anything from Dad's will, she's going to have to get a job sooner or later, so I'll bet she's trying not to think about that. But I doubt she'll want people at church finding out about it."

"Hmm," I said. It sounded as though perhaps Mrs. Montrose received the worst punishment of all—a life-long sentence of working like a commoner. "I suppose I could go," I said before I rethought it. "Sunday. To the church picnic," I added.

Amber's whole countenance brightened. "Good. We should make something. It's a potluck."

I nodded, my mind already reeling with ideas of what we could prepare, not only for Sunday, but the day after that, when I hoped to invite Amber over for another cooking lesson. And the day after that.

She'd be back in school in September, but my hope was high at the moment that I could make a habit out of being a little more social in the next couple of weeks before that happened.

A church picnic didn't sound like the most exciting afternoon in the world, but then again, delivering a casserole to a grieving family shouldn't have been nearly as exciting as it had been either.

I returned to the counter to retrieve a plate of sliced gruyere with French bread, pink lady apple, and some slivered chives. I looked over my shoulder at Amber and Hunch, who watched me, eagerly awaiting my return.

I supposed you never knew where you might find some sort of injustice to give you purpose.

And I supposed you never knew where you were going to find a new friend.

THE END

Up Next: Murder at the Church Picnic

Murder has such a sting!

If anyone had told Mallory Beck she would become Honeysuckle Grove's next amateur sleuth, she would have thought they were ten walnuts short of a brownie. Her late husband had been the mystery novelist with a penchant for the suspicious. She was born for the rotisserie, not the binoculars, and yet here she was, having just solved her first murder case. It had all started with delivering a casserole to a grieving family and finished with the help of a sarcastic teenager, a cop with kind green eyes, and a cat with a hunch.

Maybe she should have thought twice about delivering another casserole, but this one was for the potluck at the annual church picnic, and what could possibly go wrong at a picnic?

Order Murder at the Church Picnic now to continue the journey with Mallory, Amber, Alex, and Hunch at books2read.com/churchpicnic!

Turn the page for an excerpt...

Murder at the Church Picnic

Chapter One

ALMOST NINE MONTHS AND I still felt like a flake of eggshell in a bowl of yolks every time I attended a social gathering alone. At least today I'd made an extra effort to avoid any wardrobe malfunctions. Even if I did something brainless like leave the house without brushing my hair or putting on pants, I'd be meeting Amber, my new fifteen-year-old BFF, who, with any hope, wouldn't let me traipse through a public park in my underwear.

I collected the cheesy bacon and potato casserole from my kitchen and then said goodbye to Hunch, a cat with an attitude if I'd ever met one. He had recently broken his leg and dislocated his hip, so I was trying to have some grace for his bristly attitude. I compensated for his growls with my perkiest voice.

"I'll only be gone a couple of hours," I singsonged to him.

Cooper, my late husband and Hunch's true owner, used to talk to him aloud constantly. In fact, with Cooper, it had usually been less like talking to a cat and more like some kind of intelligent three-point discussion. I hadn't quite gotten comfortable with having conversations with my feline roommate yet, but then again, I didn't need his help in plotting my next mystery novel like Cooper had.

"Maybe I'll even bring Amber back with me," I told Hunch, and this earned me an uptick of his whiskers.

Amber had been visiting me almost every day since we'd solved the murder of her dad together and brought the guilty parties to justice. She always came around under the guise of a cooking lesson—I'd promised to teach her how to prepare everything from baked sourdough to ratatouille, and in fact, she'd assembled today's casserole pretty much on her own with only my instructions from the kitchen table. I'd simply popped it into the oven this morning to warm it up, filling my kitchen with the scents of savory sharp cheddar and apple-smoked bacon. Amber had wanted to make a casserole with bacon in it, and while I was as big of a fan of crispy pork as the next girl, we'd had to play around a little with the recipe so the salty flavor hadn't overpowered the rest. We'd started with nugget potatoes, but in the end, I'd suggested adding a couple of Yukon gold and Vitelotte purple potatoes to round out the flavors and add some vibrant color.

In truth, Amber probably did only show up for the cooking lessons. Me? I'd do almost anything for the company, and Hunch, I was fairly certain, would do almost anything to have someone other than me in his lair.

I left my cantankerous cat in my wake and headed for Cooper's Jeep with Amber's casserole in hand. After my husband's death, I'd driven his Jeep for months, trying to find the powerful feeling he'd claimed to have gotten from driving it, but today I chose it because of the FOR SALE sign posted prominently in the back window. I didn't often spend much of the daytime out in public, but today at the park would be the perfect opportunity to get lots of eyes on it. Surprisingly, posting the FOR SALE sign in the vehicle had made me feel the strongest I had felt in the last eight and a half months since I lost my true strength—Cooper.

I took deep breaths to steady myself on my ten-minute drive to Bateman Park. I kept telling myself it shouldn't take this much bravery to simply leave my house. It would certainly have been easy—too easy—to back out on attending the annual church picnic if I hadn't made a commitment to Amber. She had originally asked me to go with her because she didn't think her mom would be up for it. As of last night, though, it turned out her mom wanted to go, and so that left me still feeling committed, but meeting her there instead of picking her up. I hoped these solo outings would eventually get easier with time and practice

I turned the corner onto Bateman Road and discovered my next problem. Finding parking might prove as difficult as interpreting my cat's growls. The picnic was supposed to start at eleven, in lieu of today's church service, and it was already five to. I didn't like to be late, especially with someone meeting me, but nevertheless, I turned the corner and drove farther from the park in search of a space big enough for this giant gas guzzler.

I should have expected as much on such a beautiful day, but most of the time, my brain still wasn't as quick on the uptake about normal life situations as it used to be. As I wove around various back streets, I passed plenty of people walking toward the park, arms loaded with lawn chairs, blankets, and food. I recognized one couple—Marv and Donna Mayberry—which only served to increase my already racing heart. Chatting with couples after losing your spouse felt a little like driving a three-wheeled car. Marv worked long hours, so it was more common to have one-on-one time with Donna, but apparently not today. Some people strolling toward the park wore dresses and suits, and I looked down at my peach T-shirt and denim capris, wondering if there was some kind of church picnic dress code I wasn't aware of.

At least Amber would be here somewhere, and I couldn't in my wildest dreams imagine her showing up to the park in a fancy dress. I'd yet to see her in something more formal than a hoodie and cut-offs. It was just a matter of finding her. Up the next block, I finally found a space big enough for the Jeep.

Cooper had kept a couple of lawn chairs in the back of his Jeep for as long as he'd owned it. They hadn't been used in over a year, but it was time to get the creaks out of at least one of them. I'd come back for the other if Amber hadn't brought her own. Thankfully, they had backpack straps on them, so I grabbed the red one on top and slung it onto my back. Then I reached for my purse, complete with suntan lotion and bug spray, and finally for the warm casserole. The scent of salty goodness wafted up toward me as I adjusted the lid. Now that it was fresh out of the oven, the flavors had baked into one another, the melted cheese had rounded it out, and it smelled amazing.

Foot traffic thickened as I strode closer toward Bateman Park, and I kept my eyes peeled for Amber and her mom. They both had auburn hair and were both striking in different ways—Amber with her big-eyed attitude and her mom with her bouffant hairstyle—so they shouldn't be hard to spot.

Before I could find them, I rounded a small hill to get into the park, and a flurry of activity captured my attention. Tables were being assembled with food under one of the two giant park shelters, kids chased each other around the playground, and at least a dozen carnival games were being erected between the food shelter and a big open field. I'd been happy when Amber told me our contribution to the day would be food because that sounded much more up my alley than setting up and manning a ring toss or a kiddie pool fishing pond.

I surveyed the nearly one hundred heads of those either helping set up or involved in clustered conversations, but Amber and her mom weren't among them. The giant shelter on my left consisted of a large wooden gazebo with a cement floor and a half dozen picnic tables under the overhang. The tables wouldn't have nearly enough seating for our congregation, but other church members busily set up oblong tables and chairs from the church basement all around the perimeter of the shelter.

The one other shelter in the park stood about fifty feet away, and this one had rows of white chairs lined up in front of the cement area and white tulle decorating the front rafters of the shelter. A nearby table overflowed with wrapped gifts. It looked like preparations for a wedding. Two men in suits straightened the twenty-or-so rows of chairs, and many of the formally-dressed folks I'd seen on the sidewalk milled around that side of the park. I let out a breath, glad I hadn't dressed inappropriately for the picnic after all.

As I headed for the church's picnic shelter where the hot food had been placed, a nearby commotion caught my eye. Pastor Jeff was in the midst of a hushed argument with a lady I didn't recognize. She couldn't have been more than five feet tall, but what she lacked in height, she made up for with her large pregnant belly, stretched tight under a pale pink dress.

She flapped her arms to the sides, and as I moved closer, I started to make out the problem. "The bride and groom expected to have the whole park to themselves. It's their special day and they'll be here any minute! I'm their wedding planner. How do you think this is going to look for me?"

Pastor Jeff pushed his hands toward the ground and spoke in his usual calming and authoritative tone. "I understand your concern, Mrs. Winters, and I have no idea where the mix-up happened, but let's just take a deep breath and see what we can do." Pastor Jeff angled away from the pregnant lady, toward where the carnival games were being assembled. He quickly located his wife and called, "Emily? Let's try to keep all the games closer to the playground, all right?"

Between Pastor Jeff and his wife stood Marv and Donna Mayberry. They were one of the first couples Cooper and I had met at Honeysuckle Grove Community Church. Donna leaned into her husband and whispered something, likely an embellished rumor. And just like that, the giant game of telephone that always seemed to start with gossiping Donna Mayberry had begun.

"I don't care how much you move those games," the pregnant wedding planner said in an exasperated tone to Pastor Jeff. "The Bankses and the Albrights are still not going to appreciate kids running through their ceremony, and all the noise a church picnic will generate. They're not going to want these people they don't know hanging around their wedding!" She flapped her arms again. Pastor Jeff took a breath, about to speak, but she interrupted him. "Look, I don't know how the municipal office could think this park is big enough for both a wedding and a church picnic, but it's just not. I'm calling them right this second to sort this out."

I couldn't imagine the municipal office being open on a Sunday, but she pulled out a cell phone and marched away with it, not giving Pastor Jeff a chance to respond. That left our pastor staring straight at me, the only other person in the immediate vicinity. The deep grooves of his face told me he wanted to find a solution as much as the wedding planner did.

And like the last time I'd seen Pastor Jeff looking helpless, I wanted to do what I could to take that pained look off of his face.

"What can I do to help?" I asked.

Pastor Jeff wore a lavender dress shirt and khaki shorts that looked lovely together. I attributed his tidy and coordinated appearance to his wife, Emily, being here helping, instead of at her usual Sunday morning job in the church nursery. But in only one second, Pastor Jeff ran a hand through his sandy brown hair, and it stuck up in all directions, effectively ruining the put-together effect.

He shook his head. "I need to get the games moved as far away from the wedding as possible." He turned, and I took a step to follow him, but then he swung back around and said, "Actually, could you ask Sasha to gather some parents and corral the kids to keep them near the playground? That would help."

I looked to where he pointed to a lady in a long purple paisley dress. I knew the woman, or at least I had known her many years ago. She'd been my seventh-grade English teacher, back when I'd lived in Honeysuckle Grove, West Virginia, with my dad and sister more than fifteen years ago. Her hair had grown from shoulder-length to halfway down her back, and it was grayer than it had been back then, but she still clearly wore the same paisley dresses.

"You mean Ms. Mills?" I asked.

Pastor Jeff nodded, but he looked eager to rush off and speak with his secretary and the rest of the church staff to figure this out. "Yes. She takes care of our children's ministry."

If I'd had kids, perhaps I would have known that. Cooper and I had wanted kids, lots of them, but sadly, he'd been killed in a fire at one of the local banks shortly after we settled into town.

I nodded to Pastor Jeff, but still had my casserole dish in my hands, so I followed him toward his church secretary, near the food shelter, saying, "Yes, right away. I'll just put this down first."

Pastor Jeff was too concerned about his current problem to worry about me and spoke to his secretary from several feet away as he approached. "Did we not book both shelters for the picnic, Penny? Their wedding planner, Mrs. Winters, insists she has the park booked for a wedding today." He motioned to where Mrs. Winters stood angrily punching something into her phone's keyboard.

"Oh, I, um, I'm afraid I don't know." Penny Lismore was in her early twenties with bright naturally-orange hair and big blue naïve eyes. She had been the church secretary for a little less than a year. I only knew this because she had been new on the job when Cooper died, and she had made many apologies to me about not understanding procedures in booking a memorial service. Today she looked equally clueless as she picked at the side seam of her navy shorts. "Troy said he was going to book it."

I placed my casserole dish on a nearby table and looked up to where both Penny and Pastor Jeff had moved their gazes. Near the carnival games, with a clipboard in hand, stood Troy Offenbach, the treasurer of Honeysuckle Grove Community Church. He had trim blond hair, statuesque posture, and a stoic face that meant business, even at a picnic. My knowledge of Troy Offenbach was about as limited as my knowledge of Penny Lismore. He had printed off a detailed bill for Cooper's memorial service, and I had paid it.

Troy hadn't been particularly compassionate about the fact that I'd only just lost my husband a week prior, but I hadn't expected him to be. He was a numbers guy. If Cooper had taught me one thing from when I'd helped him research his mystery novels, it was that if you wanted to get a better handle on the cast of people surrounding your story, they could all quickly be reduced to certain stereotypes. Troy was all about the accounting, Penny was an employee who could follow simple instructions but wasn't much of a self-starter, and Pastor Jeff gave from the depths of such a big heart every time he came across a problem, no matter how large or small. I feared it might be the thing to break him.

"Troy!" Pastor Jeff held up an arm and beckoned his church treasurer toward him.

I took a breath and remembered the job I'd been given. Besides, did I really want to get in the middle of this situation with no easy answers? As I quick-stepped toward the kids' play park and my seventh-grade English teacher, the pregnant wedding planner moved back toward the trio of church workers looking exasperated.

"The municipal office is closed on Sundays..." was the last thing I heard as I strode away quickly.

Sasha Mills, the children's ministry coordinator, seemed no less frazzled. There had to be twenty-five kids under ten in her care, and her eyes darted from place to place as she called out short phrases such as, "Ethan, stop hitting her!" and "Amy and Zara, you're going to have to share!" and "Dominic, get down from there!" to the boy up high in the oak tree. Their parents, it seemed, were all busy helping with the picnic preparations.

"Excuse me? Ms. Mills?" I said, already feeling bad for interrupting this very busy lady. Ms. Mills had always been a bit of a softie, and if I were honest, it surprised me to see her still working with young children, ones I expected would know how to railroad over her instructions without a problem. After a couple of other called instructions, she turned to me.

"Yes?" She looked me up and down. Again, I doubted my capris and peach T-shirt. But when her gaze settled on my face, I suspected the look had more to do with a grown woman calling her Ms. Mills. It just seemed too strange to call my former teacher by her first name.

"I'm Mallory Beck—er, Vandewalker," I added, realizing she wouldn't know me by my married name. But I wanted to take up as little of her time as possible, as, out of the corner of my eye, I could tell that the little boy she'd called Ethan had started hitting the girl again. It wouldn't be long until screams ensued. "I'm not sure if you remember me..." I waved a hand. That part wasn't important. "Anyway, Pastor Jeff has come across quite an issue. Apparently, the park has been double-booked. He asked me to see if you could enlist the help of a few parents and corral the children into the playground area?"

As I said the words, Ms. Mills raised an eyebrow at me, and I realized that even if the consequences were a bomb that was about to go off or the impending end of the world, corralling this group of children was easier said than done.

"How can I help?" I asked, so at least she'd know she wasn't facing this problem on her own.

Ms. Mills took about three seconds to survey the situation, and then she pointed to a large red Rubbermaid bin near the food shelter. "Why don't you get the bin of Nerf guns? I have an idea."

As I raced to grab the bin, Ms. Mills called out the names of a few nearby parents. They came right over, and she stepped onto the wood chips of the kids' playground area and called out, "Children, listen up! The grass and the trees are lava!"

There was maybe a one-second delay, and then all of the kids who were outside of the square of the wood-chipped area looked down at their feet and raced toward the playground as Ms. Mills called out, "Three, two, one!" She pointed the mothers who had joined her around the perimeter of the playground, and they spread out.

Kids pointed and laughed at the few stragglers who hadn't made it onto the wood chips in time, but I had to hand it to Ms. Mills. She had a much better grasp on how to handle these young kids than I would have.

Most of the church men and teens followed Pastor Jeff's directions and dragged tables and games away from the wedding shelter. Other than the young kids, nobody hesitated to pitch in and help.

The Nerf gun bin was heavy, so I dragged it behind me, but only a second later, it lightened. I looked over my shoulder. Amber Montrose had grabbed the other end.

"Thank goodness you're here!" I said, now much more glad about her presence as a helper than simply so I wouldn't be standing at a social gathering alone. "The park was double-booked with a wedding. Pastor Jeff is trying to figure it out and asked that we keep the kids corralled over here."

Amber smirked—her usual reaction to most problems. Today she wore a sleeveless black T-shirt with her cut-offs that read: BUT DID YOU DIE? Her auburn curls were held back with a matching black headband. It may have been her personal style of mourning, as her dad had died less than two weeks ago.

"That should be easy," she said sarcastically.

As we arrived at the playground, Ms. Mills was already in the midst of discussing "rules" for a new game with the kids. "Nerf guns are only to be used in the wood chip area," she said. "The grass is still lava, and if I catch you with a Nerf gun on the lava, you'll lose all weapons for the rest of the day. Got it?"

The kids barely listened. At seeing the bin, all twenty-five of them barreled toward Amber and me, and only a second later, the hoard had elbowed us away from the bin so they could get in closer. Nerf guns swung up and out of the bin, and I could immediately tell this could be another accident waiting to happen.

Ms. Mills joined Amber and me near the edge of the wood chips. "This isn't going to last long, but it was all I could think of on short notice. Can you find out what's happening from Pastor Jeff?" She turned to Amber. "Can you hang out on the far side of the playground and help keep them within the boundaries, Amber?"

Amber nodded and headed that direction. I wasn't sure if Amber knew Ms. Mills from children's church or if she'd also had her as a teacher at school, but I didn't have time to ask. I turned and raced back toward the food shelter.

More guests had arrived since I'd been focused on corralling the kids, and there was a stark difference between those who were clearly here for a church picnic—in shorts and T-shirts and carrying lawn furniture—and those in dresses and suits, here for a wedding celebration.

As I skirted around picnic-goers and wedding guests to get back to the pastor and his two assistants, the pregnant wedding planner shook her head at Troy and then strode away with fists balled at her sides. I followed her eye line to three limousines that had just pulled up to the curb of the parking lot.

As if there wasn't enough to stress about, apparently the bride and groom and their entourage had arrived.

End of Excerpt. Order Murder at the Church Picnic now to read on...

Join My Cozy Mystery Readers' Newsletter Today!

Would you like to be among the first to hear about new releases and sales, and receive special excerpts and behind-the-scene bonuses?

Sign up now to get your free copy of ***Mystery of the Holiday Hustle – A Mallory Beck Cozy Holiday Mystery***.

You'll also get access to special epilogues to accompany this series—an exclusive bonus for newsletter subscribers. Sign up below and receive your free mystery:

https://www.subscribepage.com/mysteryreaders

Turn the page for a recipe from Mallory's Recipe Box...

Mallory's Old-Fashioned Butter Tarts

I LOVE TO COOK savory meals, but when I have friends around my kitchen table, discussing a case, simple, tasty treats are my go-to. This is a quick easy-to-make favorite! I like to make my own pastry dough and refrigerate it for at least 30 minutes before rolling out for baking.

<u>Tips when using your own pastry dough:</u>

Remove the dough from the fridge and roll out to 1/8" thickness.

Cut out circles with a round cookie cutter or a glass.

Gently from each round into a prepared muffin or tart tins. Prick the tarts with a fork.

Ingredients:
Homemade pastry or 12 pre-made tart shells
Butter Filling:
1/4 cup butter (melted and cooled)
1/2 cup brown sugar (lightly packed)
1/2 cup corn syrup

Pinch of salt
1 egg (beaten lightly)
1/2 teaspoon vanilla
Optional Add-ins:
1/4 cup mini chocolate chips
1/3 cup coarsely chopped pecans or walnuts

Instructions:

Prepare your favorite pie dough or store-bought tarts. Refrigerate for 30 minutes.

Pre-heat oven to 400°F. Grease and flour a 12 muffin (medium size).

Remove pastry from fridge, roll out to 1/8" thickness, and cut out with a round cookie cutter (or kitchen glass). Gently form into muffin tin. Use a small lightly floured shot glass to gently form the rounds into the tin.

Butter tart filling:

Melt the butter, let cool slightly, then add the beaten egg, vanilla, brown sugar, salt, and corn syrup stir to combine well.

Stir in the chopped pecans, walnuts, chocolate chips, or leave the filling plain.

Pour the filling into the prepared tart shells and bake for 15 minutes at 400°F, reduce heat to 350°F, and continue baking for approximately 10 - 15 minutes (until they start to brown). Let cool before serving.

Enjoy!

Storing Butter Tarts:

Store butter tarts in an airtight container and refrigerate to make them last five days. If, like me, you have regular hungry company at your table, keep them at room temperature for up to two days (if they last that long).

THE TABITHA CHASE Days of the Week Mysteries

Book 1 - Witchy Wednesday

Book 2 - Thrilling Thursday

Book 3 – Frightful Friday

Book 4 – Slippery Saturday

A Bookworm of a Suspect Mystery Anthology (Including Book 5 – Dead-end Weekend)

The Mallory Beck Cozy Culinary Capers:

Book 1 – Murder at Mile Marker 18

Book 2 – Murder at the Church Picnic

Book 3 – Murder at the Town Hall

Christmas Novella – Mystery of the Holiday Hustle

Book 4 – Murder in the Vineyard

Book 5 – Murder at the Montrose Mansion

Book 6 – Murder during the Antique Auction

Book 7 – Murder in the Secret Cold Case

Book 8 – Murder in New Orleans

Find all the Mallory Beck novels at books2read.com/denisejaden!

Collaborative Works:
Murder on the Boardwalk
Murder on Location
Saving Heart & Home
Nonfiction for Writers:
Writing with a Heavy Heart
Story Sparks
Fast Fiction

Acknowledgements

THANK YOU, READER, FOR picking up this book and giving my new little cozy series a chance. I know there are a lot of new books hitting the shelves (and virtual shelves) every day, and I am so grateful that you've given mine a chance. I hope it lives up to your expectations and that you'll follow Mallory through many more stories to come.

Thank you to my editor Angelika Offenwanger and copy-editor Sara Burgess. I feel incredibly fortunate to have your help and expertise on my side. Much appreciation to my son, Teddy Kewin, who I consider my first story editor. While I brainstorm a new novel, I always go to him with the sticky parts, or the bits that aren't feeling quite right, and he has not failed to provide me with an excellent solution every time. And while I'm on the subject of brilliantly-talented young people, thank you to Ethan Heyde, who is the artful designer of the illustrations on my covers. You have a promising career ahead of you, Ethan! Also thanks to Steven Novak of Novak Illustrations for the beautiful design work on the cover.

Thanks to my beta readers and assistant plotters, who always add great insight and see things I've missed: Shelly Wielenga, Marj Nesbitt, Norma Zenky, Lisa Green, Donna Wolff, and Danielle Lucas. Your thoughts and suggestions have helped me immensely. I'm also grateful—so very grateful—to the librarians and book bloggers who have championed this series already. Your willingness to share my work with your crowd has been instrumental.

And last but certainly not least, special thanks to Lee Strauss for all of your help in navigating the vast waters of cozy mystery writing and indie publishing. You've truly given me a life raft and I would be drowning without it.

What would a writer do without such great friends? Thank you all so much!

Denise Jaden is the author of the Mallory Beck Cozy Culinary Capers and the Tabitha Chase Days of the Week Mysteries. She is also the author of several critically-acclaimed young adult novels, and nonfiction books for writers, including the NaNoWriMo-popular guide Fast Fiction.

In her spare time, Denise acts in TV and movies and dances with a Polynesian dance troupe. She lives just outside Vancouver, British Columbia, with her husband, son, and one very spoiled cat.

Sign up on Denise's website to receive bonus content (you'll find clues in every bonus epilogue!) as well as updates on her new Cozy Mystery Series.

www.denisejaden.com

Made in the USA
Las Vegas, NV
20 November 2022